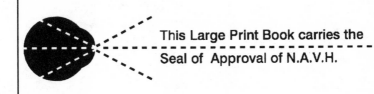

This Large Print Book carries the
Seal of Approval of N.A.V.H.

HER UNLIKELY FAMILY

HER UNLIKELY FAMILY

MISSY TIPPENS

THORNDIKE PRESS

A part of Gale, Cengage Learning

GALE
CENGAGE Learning™

Detroit • New York • San Francisco • New Haven, Conn • Waterville, Maine • London

GALE
CENGAGE Learning™

Copyright © 2008 by Melissa L. Tippens.
Thorndike Press, a part of Gale, Cengage Learning.

Thorndike Press® Large Print Christian Fiction.
The text of this Large Print edition is unabridged.
Other aspects of the book may vary from the original edition.
Set in 16 pt. Plantin.
Printed on permanent paper.

LIBRARY OF CONGRESS CATALOGING-IN-PUBLICATION DATA

Tippens, Missy.
    Her unlikely family / by Missy Tippens.
        p. cm. — (Thorndike Press large print christian fiction)
    ISBN-13: 978-1-4104-0962-1 (alk. paper)
    ISBN-10: 1-4104-0962-7 (alk. paper)
    1. Domestic fiction. 2. Large type books I. Title.
PS3620.I567H47 2008
813'.6—dc22   2008020184

Published in 2008 by arrangement with Harlequin Books, S.A.

Printed in the United States of America
1 2 3 4 5 6 7 12 11 10 09 08

We love because he first loved us.
— *1 John* 4:19

To my husband, Terry, who has read
every word I've ever written.

To my children, Nick, Tyler and
Michelle, who have cheered me along
on this journey.

To my parents,
Frank and Cellia Conley;
my sister, Mindy Winningham;
and all my extended family
who love me no matter what.

And to God for giving me the stories.

ACKNOWLEDGMENTS

Thank you to Ted Kohn, Joni Kost,
Kerry Lipscomb and Beth McLear
for research assistance.

I owe so much to my critique group,
Belinda Peterson, Maureen Hardegree
and Meg Moseley, for hours of work
on this manuscript.

I'm grateful to Georgia Romance Writers
— especially Anna DeStefano for lessons
in persistence and Sandra Chastain for
first recognizing my stories as
inspirational romance.

Thanks to The Seekers for encouragement
and laughter. And to FHL, W.O.R.D.
and the F.A.I.T.H. bloggers
for prayer and support.

Special thanks to Emily Rodmell and

Krista Stroever for making my dream of publishing come true.

CHAPTER ONE

If there was one thing Josie Miller knew, it was the smell of a rich man. And whoever had just walked into the diner smelled like Fort Knox.

She sniffed the aftershave-tinged air once again and, following her nose, popped up from behind the counter with the half-filled straw dispenser in hand. She spied the man leaning into a booth, wiping the seat with a napkin. When he sat, she got a glimpse of his face and nearly dropped the straw holder.

Black hair, black golf shirt and black mood — if the slant of his brows meant anything — said he might very well be trouble.

"I'll be right with you," she said as she spun around and hurried through the swinging door into the kitchen.

"Bogey at table one," she warned the girl at the dishwashing sink.

11

Lisa, up to her elbows in suds, gave Josie a typical teenager roll of the eyes. "Huh?"

"I think it's your uncle."

Genuine fear replaced Lisa's insolent expression. "No way!"

"Tall, dark, smells expensive?"

Lisa shook the bubbles off and dried her hands. "That could be anyone."

"Not my regular clientele."

"Does he have black hair and blue eyes?"

"Yes on the hair. I'm not sure on the eyes."

"All the girls at school say he's too gorgeous for words."

Josie opened the door a crack and took a quick glimpse. "Definitely gorgeous. In a stiff, formal kind of way." The kind of man who had never interested her. "Hurry, look. He's thumbing through his wallet."

Lisa peeked, then groaned and began to chew on her black-polished fingernail. "What am I going to do?"

Josie was wondering the same thing. She'd let down her guard after two weeks and had assumed the guy would never show up. "Go tell him you've found a job and want to stay."

"He won't let me. He'll make me go back to that school."

"I thought you said you got kicked out," Josie said.

"I did. But his little donations to fund new buildings can work wonders." She started pacing, running her fingers through her spiky green hair. "I'll die if he sends me back there."

"Calm down, Lisa. If the man's as bad as you say, surely he'll leave without a fuss."

"You don't know my uncle Michael."

No, but she knew his kind. Work and money meant everything. She could also hear the snob alert clanging in her head. "You're dealing with a pro, here." Josie smoothed her hands down the front of her uniform, then grabbed a piece of bubble gum from the shelf over the sink. "I'll give him a taste of what he'd expect from a small-time waitress, and he'll be out of here in a flash. Leave the man to me."

Michael H. Throckmorton III leaned his arms on the table, then thought better of it. He'd already had to wipe crumbs and grease off the cracked vinyl seat of this fine eating establishment, Bud's Diner.

A bald old man — Bud? — covered in sweat, wearing a filthy apron, squinted at a blaring TV perched precariously on a shelf in the corner. When a commercial came on, he turned and began raking a metal spatula across the sizzling surface of the grill.

The air, thick with the overpowering smell of grease, nearly choked Michael. A fly buzzed on the window ledge. He couldn't imagine how the place had passed health-department inspections.

Tuning out all but the task before him, he examined the outdated photograph of Lisa he always carried in his wallet. She was only fourteen at the time. A time when she used to laugh and tease him. When she used to hug him.

No time for nostalgia. It's unproductive.

Besides, Lisa's generous hugs were a lifetime ago, and so much had changed.

"What can I getcha?"

Rings adorned almost every finger — and the thumb — of a hand holding a stubby pencil poised over a pad of paper. Silver charms and beaded bracelets jangled on the woman's wrist. His gaze moved beyond multiple necklaces and gaudy dangling ear-rings to her face. A pretty face, once you got past the loud jewelry.

The petite waitress had what appeared to be pinkish-colored hair. Or was the light giving it that strange cast? He narrowed his eyes, studying the shade.

She popped her gum, then forced a smile, looking anything but friendly. "Did you want to order?"

"Bottled water, please."

"No bottles. Just tap."

He needed to order something. Anything. The latest report from the private investigator led right to this greasy spoon.

"You know, we scored a hundred percent on our last inspection." She pointed her pencil at a certificate on the wall by the door.

Though he was perfectly within his rights as a customer to worry about such things, his face heated. He hadn't meant to offend with his hesitancy. "Fine. I'll have a glass of ice water with lemon. And . . ." He flipped open a menu and ordered the first item that caught his attention. "A grilled chicken sandwich with lettuce and tomato."

"Fries with that?"

"No, thank you."

She grinned. "Where're you from?" Then she snapped her gum again.

If she would stop that annoying chewing, she'd have a nice mouth.

Her brown eyes sparked, as if she could read his mind.

"I'm from Charleston," he finally answered.

"So you're in Gatlinburg on vacation?"

He nailed her with his oft-used intimidating expression, the one that cowed most people. "Actually, I'm looking for my niece. Lisa Throckmorton." He showed her the picture. "Have you seen her?"

"I can't really say." She didn't flinch. The woman was either good at hedging, or she was telling the truth. And she obviously wasn't easily intimidated.

"This photo is two years old," he said. "She threatened to dye her hair green the last time I talked to her. I have no idea whether or not she followed through."

"So what did you tell her?"

"Pardon me?"

"When she threatened about her hair. What did you say?"

He ran his hand through his own hair, determined to get the waitress back on track. "Never mind that. She's a runaway."

"Oh, that's too bad."

He scooted the picture across the table. "She's been missing nearly two weeks, but we think she may be close by. I plan to find her and take her home."

"Take her home, huh? How old is she?"

"Sixteen."

The waitress's eyes filled with suspicion. "Not quite old enough to be off on her own. Why'd she run away?"

If he didn't know better, he would think her tone held accusation that he was a poor guardian. But she wouldn't have any idea he was raising his sister's daughter.

"It's really none of your business," he said. "She has a family who loves her and wants her back."

"So you won't answer my question, huh?"

The impertinent waitress had just about frayed his last nerve. Not what he needed while wasting precious time. He glanced at his watch, thinking for a split second of the weekly loan committee meeting he was missing. "No, I won't answer it."

The woman's gaze bore into his as if she were trying to decipher his thoughts. The air between them crackled with unspoken censure, and for a moment he feared she could see through to his worry that he was failing his sister yet again, even now, after her death.

He shook off the crazy, morbid thought. "So, have you seen my niece?"

"She may have passed through." She stuck the pencil behind her ear. "Gotta put your order in."

She walked to the end of the counter, leaned across it and yelled, "Grilled chick, dressed," to the man with the shiny forehead and five-o'clock shadow. The sweaty cook acknowledged the order with a jerk of his head and then eyed the waitress; some kind of message seemed to pass between them.

Michael sat back in the booth, crossed his arms and settled in. He wasn't going anywhere until he found out if the message had anything to do with Lisa. She wasn't going to spend one more night alone on the streets. He would find her, even if it meant having to eat another meal in this dive.

After Josie delivered Michael's water, she made a beeline to the kitchen.

Lisa stood beside the door, chewing on her fingernail. "What did he say?"

"He's searching for one Lisa Throckmorton, *sixteen*-year-old runaway." She arched her brow at the supposed recently turned eighteen-year-old. "You showed me a fake driver's license."

"I'm sorry. I was afraid you'd send me back if you knew."

"You're right about that. I could probably go to jail for harboring a minor."

Lisa squinched up her nose. "You didn't tell, did you?"

"No. But I was tempted. You'd better not lie to me again."

"I won't. I promise." She held her fingers up in a Girl Scout promise. "Did he leave yet?"

"No. He ordered a sandwich."

"Great. Now I'm stuck here. I was invited to a gallery opening tonight up at the craft school."

"This is serious, Lisa. I really should tell him you're here. He must be worried sick."

"Please, please, pleeease don't. I guarantee you he's not worried. He'd rather be off counting his money right now."

Josie spun her Mickey Mouse watch around — 7:00 p.m. "I want you to tell me the truth about your uncle. He didn't seem like the monster you've painted him to be. He came all the way from Charleston looking for you, after all."

"I told you before. He doesn't want me. He shipped me off to boarding school a year ago, only a week after my mom died."

"Well, maybe he thinks that's best. The school has a really good reputation."

Lisa's eyes brightened, and she blinked away tears. "He doesn't want me, okay? I heard him tell my grandmother the day after the funeral."

Josie wanted to shake the man. "Does he call you or visit?"

"He always cancels. He's too busy. And I hate that place."

A sixteen-year-old girl whose mother had just died shouldn't be shipped off to boarding school. She should be with her family.

And Josie knew all too well about craving attention from family.

"What's your uncle like? Not as a parent. As a person."

Lisa rolled her eyes. "He's always on the straight and narrow. Churchgoing. Law-abiding. Serious." She thought for a second. "He, like, owns the bank. He's worked there since he was five or something."

"Sounds like a good role model to me."

"You promised me, Josie." She backed away, as if heading for the door. "If you tell him, I'm out of here. 'Cause he'll send me right back to that horrible place and all those snobby kids who won't have anything to do with me."

"And you've told him how they exclude you?"

"I think I mentioned it."

"You think?"

"I did tell him about the three girls on my floor who've spread lies about me. But he didn't believe me, because he knows their parents really well."

Well, that decided it. Josie wasn't about to turn the girl over to an uncle who would deny a problem and pack her off to school with kids who mistreated her.

Then again, she probably shouldn't take Lisa's word for it. Josie would stall answering his questions about Lisa's whereabouts until she could find out for herself what kind of guardian he was.

A serious, law-abiding banker, huh? He would be as easy to read as Bud's menu.

Michael finished the last bite of his sandwich and had to admit the chicken was tender and spiced to perfection. However, after the exhausting day he'd spent driving without stopping to eat, anything would have tasted good.

The waitress with Josie printed on her name tag jangled as she hurried toward his table, waving a slip of paper. "I've got your check right here."

She certainly was trying to rush him out the door.

He wasn't budging. "I think I'd like some dessert. What's the chef making today?"

The woman snorted a laugh. "Chef? If Bud over there is a chef, I'll eat my orthopedic shoes."

He glanced down at the old-lady shoes, which suited her personality about as well as a tiara on her head would. "Believe me, Josie, I had already deduced he wasn't trained at Le Cordon Bleu."

She smiled, but the tilt of her brows made her seem confused. She touched her name tag. "You know my name. What's yours?"

"Michael Throckmorton."

"Well, you're a funny man, Mike."

"It's Michael. I've never been called Mike."

"But Michael sounds so stuffy."

"Maybe I *am* stuffy. Now, what's on the dessert menu today?"

With a mischievous gleam in her eye, she parked one hip on the edge of his table, leg swinging, and pointed to the far wall. "The dessert menu's on that chalkboard. Same today as yesterday and every day for the past year or so. Pecan pie, apple pie or chocolate cake?"

"Make it apple, with black coffee."

"I figured you for an apple-pie man. Coming right up."

Now what was that supposed to mean? "Would you please ask Bud to come take a look at this picture of Lisa when he gets a moment?"

"He's real busy. But I'll try." She shoved her pencil, not behind her ear this time, but into her bird's nest of a hairdo, then moved to wait on another table where she flirted with two men in dirty work clothes.

In observing her at a distance, he decided that somehow, miraculously, she equaled a whole lot more than the sum of her parts.

Extreme jewelry, plus funky hair and rubber-soled shoes equaled . . . attractive waitress.

How could that possibly be?

When Josie returned with Michael's pie and coffee, she slid into the booth across from him. She blew a pink bubble, then popped it with a loud snap. "So, tell me about you and your niece. Are you helping her parents search for her?"

He lifted Lisa's photograph and stared at the innocent, trusting smile. A smile that used to come so easily before her mother's drinking had gotten out of hand.

"My sister, Patricia, was a single mom. She died in a car accident a year ago."

"Oh, no. Don't tell me it was a drunk driver."

"Yes. Her." *Way to go, Throckmorton. Tell her your life history, why don't you?*

His unintentional revelation was greeted with silence. And a pitying look — which he detested.

"Anyway, she specified in her will that I be named guardian," he added.

"Why'd she pick you?"

He bristled. "Why not me?"

"Well, you appear to be single." She waggled her left ring finger. "No ring."

Yes, he was single. Definitely single since

Gloria had dumped him. "An unmarried man can be a suitable guardian."

"I didn't say you were unsuitable. I'm just wondering why she chose you."

Josie was acting a little too interested. As if she was stalling.

The longer this woman gave him the runaround, the more likely it was he would be stuck in Gatlinburg, missing his appointment with Tom Mason. And Throckmorton's Bank needed Mason's company to take out that construction loan.

He checked his watch. "You know, I really want to find her and get back to Charleston. I have an important meeting tomorrow. Do you have any idea where she could be?"

"So this is all about getting back to your *important* meeting, huh?"

He sighed. This woman was impossible. Since when was it a crime to work hard? "No. It's about making sure my niece is safe. About getting her back to school — and round-the-clock supervision — where she belongs before she makes a stupid mistake." Like her mother made sixteen years ago.

"What kind of mistake?"

"Some of her friends thought she might have left with an older boy. A troublemaker."

Josie thought about her one encounter

with the troublemaker boyfriend and said a quick prayer of thanks that the creep had ditched Lisa and hit the road — even if he had "borrowed" her car.

She figured another prayer for guidance wouldn't be a bad idea either since Michael Throckmorton didn't seem as awful as Lisa had made him out to be. In fact, he seemed downright concerned. Except for wanting to get back for a meeting. That bothered her.

But maybe she should at least let him know Lisa was safe.

But then Lisa would feel betrayed and might run again.

What a mess.

"You know, Mike, if you'll hang around until I'm off tonight, I might be able to help you."

His all-business, I'm-in-a-hurry-to-get-out-of-here scowl lit with a hint of hope. "I knew it. You do know where Lisa is."

"Order's up," Bud called.

What should she do? Mike obviously cared for his niece. Maybe he just didn't know how to show it. "Okay, I admit I've met her, and I can tell you she's safe. But she doesn't want to see you."

He winced at the truth. "She's made that fairly clear."

Bud impatiently clanged the little service bell and nodded toward a customer. "Hamburger's getting cold."

"Look, I need to get back to work. I'm pulling a double, so I don't get off till ten."

She hopped up and went to pick up the order, but when she turned to take it to the table, she glimpsed the back of Mike's broad back as he disappeared through the swinging door into the kitchen.

By the time she caught up to him, he stood alone in the middle of the spick-and-span room. Lisa was nowhere in sight.

"She's not here." He sounded deflated.

"No. But like I said, she's safe."

He zeroed in on the exit leading to the alley. "If I don't find her, I'll meet you outside at ten. But I expect some answers." In four strides of his long legs, he was out the door, his head snapping left and right to search the darkening alley.

Bud stuck his head into the kitchen, saw the intruder was gone and said, "She left with Brian after he delivered the bread."

"Do you have any idea where they went?"

"No."

A flutter of panic beat against Josie's chest. "What if she ran again?"

A worried look deepened his wrinkles, but he shrugged. "The girl's your mission project. Not mine." The door flapped closed as he went back to the dining room and his grill.

Josie wondered if protecting Lisa had been the right thing to do. Instinct had told her the girl needed some time away from peer pressure, family pressure, and the burden wealth could put on a person — just as Josie had needed at that age. Lisa needed time to figure out who she was and what she wanted out of life.

But Josie had thought she was dealing with an unwanted eighteen-year-old. Now she had to find a way to prevent the girl from running away again while being responsible to the hunky uncle. Maybe she could hold him off until she talked to Lisa — providing Lisa showed up at home that night.

Lord, I thought You sent Lisa to me like You sent the other runaways. I thought You wanted me to help her. But I don't have any business keeping her from an uncle who seems to care about her.

God had sent Lisa to her for a reason. She simply had to figure out what that reason could be.

Michael hunkered down in his car. The late March temperature had dropped and couldn't be over forty. Not exactly what he'd dressed for earlier in the day, back before he'd known he would have to hang around to deal with a frustrating waitress as the only link to his niece.

He had a view of the front of the diner and of the alley leading from the back. So far, he'd only seen customers come and go. No sign of Lisa.

He pushed the button to light his watch. Eight past ten and still no sign of Josie, either.

The woman certainly worked hard. Unless, of course, she'd spent her time warning Lisa not to come back to the diner. The fact that Josie had misled him earlier didn't bode well for how truthful she would be tonight.

The fact that Lisa had told Josie she didn't want to see him didn't bode well either.

A sigh escaped from some weary place deep inside. How was he supposed to deal with a teenager who was so rebellious she broke every school rule twice? Surely the school, with female role models like her teachers, was better than his bachelor home. Once again, he would have to find a way to get Lisa reinstated.

He steeled himself for her objections. He would find her and take her back where she belonged. Maybe someday she would thank him for it.

The door of the diner opened, and Josie, without any wasted movement, walked toward his car. Before he knew it, she had climbed in and shut the door.

"Hi, Mike. Nice night."

"Would you care to join me?"

"I thought you'd never ask." Light from a streetlamp spilled into the car, illuminating her sassy smirk.

He stopped himself from telling her she had a nice smile, even though she did have a very nice smile. Instead, he sat in silence, turning to the quiet neighborhood outside, remembering the more touristy area a few blocks away where shops sold handmade candles, homemade fudge and funnel cakes. Why would a teenager head to this town?

When he recalled the many wedding chapels in the area, his gut clenched. "I'm not too late to keep her from trying to marry the punk, am I?"

"No. The guy dumped her. But —"

"So you do know about him." Anger pushed away the chill in the air. "What else have you kept from me?"

"It's not like I —"

His cell phone rang. He unclipped it from his belt. Caller ID showed it was the investigator. "Throckmorton."

"They traced your niece's car to a town in North Georgia," the man said. "A young couple was seen getting out. We're not sure if it's Lisa. The female's hair is black."

"Did you call the police?"

"A patrol car is on its way now."

"Georgia, huh? What about credit-card activity?"

"None since the day she disappeared."

Michael drummed his thumb on the steering wheel. "Okay. Thanks."

"I'll call as soon as we find her."

Snapping the phone closed, he watched Josie. She had her legs crossed, foot jiggling. She spun her bracelets around her wrist. Either the woman couldn't sit still or she was nervous.

None of this made sense. Was Josie lying? He had thought for sure he was on Lisa's trail. He prayed he was right.

"So that call was about Lisa?" Josie asked.

"It was the P.I. I hired to locate her."

"What did you find out?"

"He says Lisa may be in Georgia with a guy. Her car's there, anyway."

Josie sat up at attention, then frowned. "The creep took her car. So I assume he's with someone else."

"Took her car? Why didn't she report the theft?"

"Lisa wanted to wait. She thinks he'll bring it back."

"Could he have come back for Lisa today?"

"Well, she was here at dinnertime. But she lit out once she saw you."

He breathed in through his nose, trying to control the urge to yell. "You mean to tell me she was at the diner, and while you chatted and stalled, she snuck away again?"

"No, I — Do you think she could have gotten to that town in Georgia in the three hours since you got here?"

"I have no idea."

She clicked her fingernails on the leather interior, then opened her door. "Let me run and get a phone directory, then make some calls."

He reached over her to close the door. "Wait just a moment."

Josie, who'd been jerking him around all evening, was trying to make an awfully sudden exit. And now she acted as if she feared Lisa had run away again? Well, he would bet the last dollar in Throckmorton's Bank that Lisa wasn't in Georgia with her car.

"I want you to tell me the truth, and tell me right now," he said.

31

"I have told you the truth. She's most likely still here. Then again, I'm not positive." She reached for the door handle. "Let me try to find her and talk her into meeting with you."

"No. You've had your chance. Tell me where to look."

"Come on, Mike, I promised her. You're putting me in a tough position."

"If you think you're in a tough position now, wait until I have you arrested for kidnapping."

CHAPTER TWO

Think, Josie, think.

Mike looked so imposing in the dimly lit car. All angles and shadows. If she hadn't heard from his niece that he was a law-abiding citizen, she would be pulling out her pepper spray right about now.

She forced a carefree laugh. "Kidnapping? Now you're being ridiculous."

"I'm dead serious. You're keeping a minor away from her legal guardian."

"Okay, I admit I was uncooperative at first. But she'd told me she was eighteen. And, for the record, I didn't have anything to do with her sneaking out of the diner this evening."

With his dark brows drawn together, he glared at her. "You could have told me as soon as you noticed her missing."

"She's not necessarily missing. She said something about having plans tonight. I imagine she'll show up later either here or at my house."

"She knows where you live? Let's go check there."

Josie tentatively touched his forearm, surprised at the warmth against her cold fingers. "I can't betray her. I promised I'd protect her from you."

"Protect?" He jerked his arm away. "What on earth did she tell you? That I beat her?"

Josie hesitated.

"Come on. I would never do a thing to hurt Lisa. I just want her safely at school."

"Mike, she'll come around eventually. But right now you need to do what's best for Lisa."

"I know what's best for my own niece."

"I'm not so sure about that." Before he could argue, she said, "I need time to talk her into meeting with you. Promise me you won't ambush her, or she may truly run again."

He gripped the steering wheel so tightly it was a wonder it didn't bend. He shook his head and exhaled. "Why are you doing this for a runaway teenager — a stranger?"

"Because I was in her shoes once."

"You ran away?" he said as if surprised.

"Yep. Twice."

"Did your parents find you?"

"They did the first time. The second time,

I had just graduated from high school, so they didn't do anything about it."

As he digested her story, she relaxed against the seat and said, "I guess I should head home and wait. Lisa has about two hours before her midnight curfew."

"Curfew? Is she living with you?"

Forget relaxing. She had almost let that piece of information slip. If she told him yes, he would be sitting on her doorstep around the clock. "She's been staying somewhere safe. I keep tabs on her. That's all I'm saying for now."

He tried the bending-the-steering-wheel trick one more time. The man oozed tension.

Of course, she would, too, in the same situation.

"You know, I hate to sit and wait," he said. "If you're wrong about her whereabouts, she could be getting farther away by the minute."

"There's a possibility she's at the nearby craft school. I'll drive up there and make sure."

He slowly turned his head and stared at Josie with his night-darkened blue eyes. "Why couldn't you have said that as soon as you came out here?"

His intensity sent little sparks of awareness along her nerve endings. Which was absolutely crazy. His type usually made her want to shudder. "I had to make sure I could trust you," she sputtered.

"Trust, Josie? I assure you, *you* can trust *me*."

His inflection said exactly what he thought of her. He would understand her wariness, though, if only he knew how a rich, domineering man had let her down before.

Her conscience pricked her for being judgmental. *Lord, help me not to compare Mike with my dad, not to judge him. But most of all, protect Lisa. And please, please, let her be at the craft school.*

Josie continued to plead with God as she directed Mike to park at the entrance to the campus. He'd insisted on coming along. As she'd discovered, when Mike insisted, a person didn't have much choice.

"Wait here. I'll walk up and look in the gallery," she said.

"It's after ten. I would think it would be closed."

"If I don't find her in the gallery, I'll see if I can find Brian's truck."

Mike thunked his head against the headrest and closed his eyes. "Brian?"

"The bread delivery guy. Bud said she left

with him."

With a not-at-all-happy laugh, he shook his head. "I'll give you ten minutes. Then I'm driving up to take a look around."

"Come on, Mike. If you chase her down now, nothing will have changed. She'll just run again — if not tonight, then another day. Don't blow it with impatience."

He leaned closer, right in her face, and boy, did he smell good.

"You haven't begun to see my impatience, Josie. Ten minutes. Not one minute longer."

She moved closer until her nose almost touched his. "I'm not some peon crawling to you, begging for a loan."

Without moving an inch away from her challenge, he said, "Ready, set . . ." Then, somehow, his watch beeped. ". . . Go."

As much as she would love to argue with the maddening man, she resisted and slung the door open. She jumped out and started running up the drive. *Forget your pride, Josie. Think of Lisa.*

Huffing and puffing, she stopped at the main building, but it was dark. A trip around the building revealed music playing up the hill at one of the visiting artists' cottages.

She followed the sound and about collapsed in relief when she heard Lisa's voice.

Now she had to somehow send Lisa home without giving away the fact that Mike was only two hundred yards away.

A brisk walk to the porch of one of the houses found Lisa, Brian and a group of students talking over the strains of jazz.

"Hi," Josie said.

"Josie! What are you doing here?" Lisa's gaze darted around, no doubt looking for Mike.

"I came to tell you to get on back to the house."

"What about my uncle?"

"We'll talk about him when you get there."

"Curfew isn't until twelve."

"I just changed it to ten-thirty."

"But it's that time now."

"Then I suggest you get going."

"But, Josie —"

"As long as you're under my roof, I expect you to play by my rules." *Please don't let this backfire!*

Lisa looked at her new friends and shrugged. "I guess I'll see ya later. Thanks for telling me about the gallery opening. It was awesome."

"Hey, anytime," a young woman said. "I hope you'll consider taking some classes."

"Sure." Lisa glanced at Josie guiltily. "When I'm old enough." She took the hand of the tall, lanky kid next to her. "Come on, Brian."

"Brian, I expect you to take her directly home," Josie said.

"Yes, ma'am."

As dignified as she could, Josie traipsed down the hill, then started into a full run as soon as she was out of sight. She met Mike's headlights halfway up the drive and stepped in the middle of the road, putting up her hand to tell him to halt.

Once he stopped, she hurried to the passenger's side and climbed in. "She's here. Back up and go out the way we came in before she sees you, or she's liable to tell Brian to head to the state line."

Michael looked ahead up the road and thought for a moment about staying put, blocking the drive.

"If we're lucky, they'll take another minute or two to get to Brian's truck." Josie breathed heavily, her hair a wild curly mess falling out of confinement.

"How do I know you really saw her at all?"

She growled her irritation. "If my running all the way up there was for nothing, then I may just . . ." She growled again.

Josie might have a point. He didn't want to risk scaring Lisa away. He'd have to believe the crazy woman beside him.

He backed the car up, then squealed out of the parking lot.

"Hey. Watch it," she said. "You might get your Beemer dusty or something."

He let off the gas. "I'm sorry. I don't usually drive so carelessly."

"I suspected as much."

"It's just so frustrating to get this close and not see her."

"She'll meet you tomorrow. I won't take no for an answer."

Josie didn't seem to be jesting. "You'll do that for me?"

"I'll do it for *Lisa.* Whether she realizes it or not, she needs you."

"Exactly. She needs my influence to get her reinstated in school where she has stability, where she has female role models."

"I said she needs you — your love — not the substitute you're trying to provide."

Love. He almost laughed out loud. Hadn't Gloria, as she'd returned his great grandmother's engagement ring, told him he wasn't even capable of loving? And what about his own sister? Patricia had certainly made her opinion of his love perfectly clear on the night she'd died.

Love? A stab of guilt knocked him deeper into his seat. What could he possibly offer Lisa besides a prestigious private school, a fine college education and a position at the bank?

"I'll take you home," he said. "I'm holding you to your word about tomorrow."

"My car's at the diner."

"You know, I'm struggling with leaving this all in your hands. Do you promise you won't help her escape tonight?"

"Of course I won't. Trust me."

In his world, trust was only secured once there was a solid, no-loopholes contract signed. Somehow, he didn't see her signing anything at the moment. He arched one brow at her, but she merely smiled. Which didn't reassure him at all.

"Mike, you never mentioned Lisa's father. Why isn't he the guardian?"

"Lisa's father has never been in the picture. He and my sister never married."

"Then it must have been really hard for Lisa when her mother died."

Difficult for Lisa, yes. But at least she didn't have to live with the guilt of being at fault. He was the one who'd said horrid things that had upset Patricia that night. "I don't think she's fully dealt with Patricia's death. Other than with excessive rebellion."

"I imagine it's been tough trying to love a troublemaking teenager."

He clenched his teeth to keep from griping about how tough. "We've had our rough spots."

"Why did she run away? Honestly."

He hesitated. Of course, Josie probably knew the whole story. Lisa tended to tell things like they were. "She doesn't like boarding school. She wants to live with me, but I can't take care of her. I'm at the bank twelve hours a day, and I travel."

"It's not like she's a toddler. She could be home a couple of hours a day by herself. You could even send her to her grand-parents or hire someone to help."

"She's landed in too much trouble to be left to her own devices. And my parents can't take on that responsibility." He stopped at a red light. "As far as hiring someone to function as a sort of nanny, well, I didn't like any of the candidates I interviewed."

"Maybe you should make some adjust-ments to your schedule for the welfare of your niece."

As he turned up the street to the diner, he fought the temptation to defend himself. Ultimately, his schedule was none of her business. "I make decisions as I see fit, and I'd appreciate it if you'd keep your advice to yourself from now on." He motioned to a lone parked car. "Is that your vehicle?"

42

"Yes, that's my heap of junk. And I'll try to keep my opinions to myself."

Try was the operative word.

"How am I going to be sure Lisa is secure for the night?" he asked.

"Give me your cell-phone number, and I'll call if she doesn't show up at my house."

"Ah, I see. So she is staying at your house."

A smile spread across her face. "Man, Mike, you're good."

"What can I say?"

She pulled a scrap of paper out of her pocket. "Do you have a pen? I need your number."

There was no way he would go to bed tonight without catching a glimpse of Lisa. "How about I follow you home? I won't let Lisa see me."

"That won't be necessary, Mike."

"Michael."

"That won't be necessary, Mike." She smiled so sweetly it made it difficult to stand firm.

Difficult, but not impossible. "Oh, yes it will."

Michael followed Josie to within a block of her house. After she went in the front door and flashed the porch light, their prearranged signal that Lisa was there, he pulled his car closer.

A light came on in a side window. Maybe he could take a quick look, just to confirm Lisa was really there. And that they weren't packing her bags.

He parked, got out, then crept around the corner of the tiny, vinyl-siding home. Strangely, it appeared to be pink in the glow of the streetlights.

Pink hair, pink uniform, pink house. Strange woman.

After surveying the height of the window, he quickly grabbed an empty metal garbage can from the neighbor's yard to stand on, then eased along the wall of Josie's house. A cat darted out of the bushes, scaring the life out of him. He nearly dropped the trash can.

But he carried on with his mission and set the can upside down, then climbed up, standing on the edges to keep the bottom from denting in. He rose up on his toes. As he reached the window, he realized it was raised about two inches. Voices carried out the opening.

Jackpot!

"I can't believe you let him follow you here," Lisa said in an angry whisper, as if he might somehow be near enough to hear.

"He didn't exactly give me any choice."

44

Josie had her back to him, but he could see the top of Lisa's head. Green head.

Though relief at finally seeing her eased the knot in his stomach, irritation that she had carried out her hair-coloring threat sparked through him. It would be one more battle Lisa would wage with her grandmother.

Lisa moved to the side. Her hair wasn't only green. It also looked as if a lawn mower had gotten hold of it. "You promised you'd get rid of him, Josie."

"That was before I realized he's not as bad as you said he was."

"But you didn't try. You sat right down and started chatting with him at the diner like he was some long-lost friend."

"And he wasn't even scared off by my interrogation or gum-snapping small-time waitress act."

"Scared off? He probably hasn't had a date since snooty ol' Gloria told him to take a hike. The poor guy must be desperate."

Incensed, Michael said, "I beg your pardon."

The screams of the two women startled him, but he managed to stay balanced. Josie, on the other hand, dropped to the floor, and Lisa practically dove under the bed.

"It's only me, the desperate one," he said.

Josie hopped up and fully raised the window. "You . . . You Peeping Tom! I should call the police."

"Go right ahead. I'll tell them you're hiding a minor here. For all I know, you kidnapped her."

He squinted, peering through the screen into the tiny bedroom. "Speaking of the minor . . . Lisa, come out from under there."

Silence.

"Lisa . . ."

"Oh, give it up, Lisa," Josie said. "Come on out. We're busted."

"And so are you, buddy," said a gravelly voice behind Michael. "Police. Put your hands up."

Josie had to fight the incredulous laugh that nearly bubbled out of her. It wasn't very often the president of a bank found himself in Mike's position. She pressed her face against the screen and found a frequent patron of the diner and member of her church. "Hello, Officer Fredrickson."

"You okay here, Josie? Your neighbor called saying someone was sitting in a car casing out your house. Do you know this man?"

Mike glared at her, and she bit her lower lip to keep from grinning.

"I don't really *know* him. . . ." This would

46

be one way to get Mike off Lisa's back. But did she dare?

"So, do you want to press charges against this pervert?"

"Pervert? This is ridiculous. My name is Michael Throckmorton. My niece is in there." He leaned his face closer. "Tell the man, Josie. You do remember what we talked about?"

Yes, the supposed kidnapping. She couldn't risk it. "I actually met him today, Officer. And his niece is here in, uh, on the floor."

Lisa slung the yellow-flowered bedspread back and scooted out from under the bed. She approached the window, her furious gaze spearing first Josie, then Mike.

"Is this your uncle, Miss?"

She jammed her hands on her hips. "Yes."

"Then what's he doing out here peeking in?" the policeman asked.

"It's not something I do every day," Michael said through clenched teeth, scowling at Josie. "Can I put my hands down now and explain?"

"Sure, if you'll hop off there and show me some ID."

While Mike complied, Josie coaxed Lisa to go outside with her. They joined Mike on the lawn as the officer checked his license with a flashlight.

Josie figured she'd better not push him any further. "You can go, Officer Fredrickson. We were about to discuss his niece."

"You're sure? I won't leave if you're not totally comfortable."

Recalling the full name printed on the business card Mike had left at the diner with Bud, she knew she would never be totally comfortable around one Michael H. Throckmorton III. "We're fine here. Just a misunderstanding."

"Okay. You can relax now, buddy. Call if you need anything, Josie." He pressed the button on his shoulder radio to call the station and lumbered away.

Mike stood nearly nose-to-nose with Josie. "Let's go in the house. Now."

Each word was its own sentence. The man meant business.

Well, she meant business, too. She jabbed at his nose with her forefinger. "Talk to me in that tone of voice and I'll call the cop back over here."

"Go right ahead. I'll throw around the word *kidnapping* this time." He tried to peer around Josie. "Lisa, get packed. You're coming with me right now."

"No."

"I won't take no for an answer."

48

"Then you'll have to drag me kicking and screaming. What will the neighbors think about that? Huh?"

Michael thought his blood pressure might blow out the top of his head. Never in his life had he been this frustrated. There was only one solution.

He barreled toward the front of the house. "Officer Fredrickson!"

The man heard him and rolled down his window. "Yes, Mr. Throckmorton?"

"I want to press charges."

"What on earth for?"

"Kidnapping, against Josie."

"Kidnapping?"

"Or delinquency against my niece. Whichever will get a runaway sixteen-year-old home the quickest."

Michael had to hurry each step to keep up with the irate, stomping pace of Lisa.

"I cannot *believe* you," she raged in her staccato fury — the same words she'd repeated a dozen times on the way to the police precinct.

He was beginning to regret his hasty decision. It didn't look as if it would work in his favor. Especially since Josie had offered herself so the cop wouldn't haul Lisa in to the station.

Michael reached around Lisa to open the door to the building, but she grabbed the handle and flung it outward, nearly hitting him in the face.

"I just can*not* believe you did this to her."

As he started to ask a man at the front desk where to find Josie, Lisa squealed her name and ran into an adjoining room.

The "prisoner" sat perched on the edge of Officer Fredrickson's desk, her busy foot swinging, while the man laughed at something she'd said.

She didn't look too traumatized, yet Lisa threw herself at Josie as if Josie had been abducted and tortured for a month.

"I'm okay, Lisa. We were just talking."

"You mean they didn't, like, lock you up with murderers?"

"You may be watching a little too much TV, darlin'," the older officer said in a kind voice. "The first thing we have to do is fill out form after form."

Lisa's eyes teared up. Michael assumed it was from relief. He hadn't realized having Josie arrested would frighten his niece so much.

Lisa grabbed the officer's arm. "Josie didn't do anything wrong. She never made me stay. She's been helping me."

Lisa turned to Michael. Her anger seemed

50

to have vanished, and her eyes pleaded with him. "I don't ask for much. But I'm asking now. Tell them to let her go." She swallowed. "Please." It came out in a choked whisper.

How could he refuse?

"We haven't filed any paperwork yet," the officer said.

Josie patted his niece and gave Michael a mother-bear look. "All you've managed to do is scare her to death. You're not helping yourself a bit."

With a wave of his hand, he said, "Fine. I won't press charges."

Instead of rushing into his arms and thanking him, Lisa glared daggers at him, took Josie's hand, then tugged her back to the entrance as if racing away before he changed his mind.

"Josie's a good woman," the cop said. "You can trust her with your niece. Our church has referred a couple of runaways to her. She's worked wonders."

He was coming to the same conclusion himself, but didn't have to like the fact. Michael nodded to the man. "Thank you, sir. Sorry to have caused you any trouble this evening."

"No trouble at all. Added a little excitement to an otherwise boring night."

Michael's night had been far from boring.

And what now? Waiting in his car were two indignant females.

"For the last time, no," Lisa said.

Michael sat across Josie's coffee table — actually it was an old crate painted bright yellow — from his niece. They were at a standoff. He had said come home, she'd said no. Repeatedly.

There seemed to be no middle ground. And he was exhausted.

Against all odds, when they had arrived back at Josie's house, she had invited him in to talk to Lisa. Since he had survived the ride home without any violent outbursts, he had assumed Lisa had settled down and would be reasonable.

Apparently, she hadn't, and wouldn't. Out of desperation, he said, "Your grandmother said to tell you that you need to be back in school."

With a little snort and sarcastic laugh, she said, "Oh, okay. Then give me five minutes to pack." Of course she made no move to cooperate. As she sulked, slouching in a tattered blue recliner, he studied the room. It was clean, but definitely not tidy. The decor was modern thrift shop.

Then he noticed the walls. It seemed every inch of space was covered by the most eclectic collection of framed prints he'd ever seen. Watercolors, oils, photographs. Landscapes, flowers, portraits, posters, strange and unidentifiable —

"Here's your Coke," the art collector herself said as she walked into the room from the kitchen.

He pulled his attention away from the weird sketch. Except for that particular one, he rather liked the feel of the room.

She handed him his drink. "I see you've been admiring my artwork."

He glanced at her sheepishly. "Yes."

"Just so you know, every piece has sentimental value."

"Really?

"I know what you're thinking," she said, eyes sparking.

"I'm sure you don't."

"You can't believe I have such a hodgepodge hung up all over the place."

"No, actually —"

"You don't have to deny it, Uncle Michael. I could see it on your face, too." With her forefinger, Lisa pushed up the tip of her nose. "All the Throckmortons are such snobs."

"Lisa, don't talk to your uncle that way," Josie said.

Michael stopped with the can halfway to

his lips. The spit-fire waitress was full of surprises. He would have expected her to agree.

Lisa appeared as surprised as he was. "I can't believe you're taking his side, Josie."

"I'm not taking sides at all. You just need to learn to respect your uncle." She sat on the opposite end of the sofa from Michael. "Now, have you two solved anything?"

"No," he said. "It seems we're at an impasse."

Josie kicked off her work shoes and wiggled her stockinged toes. "Can I make a suggestion?"

"Go for it," Lisa said. "Anything that'll help him see I'm never going back to that awful school where the teachers try to make us cookie-cutter copies of each other."

He pointed his finger at Lisa. "They're trying to make you, at a minimum, fit for polite society."

"Mike, talking like that isn't going to help one bit," Josie warned.

Lisa grinned as if she'd won the skirmish. But he knew Josie was right.

"Speaking of the school . . ." Josie said. "Has Lisa told you about the kids mistreating her?"

"She claimed some girls on her floor have spread outrageous rumors about her. But I know their families and find it highly un-likely."

"You don't believe me."

"Maybe the girl that informed you of the situation misunderstood. Or maybe you misunderstood."

"I'm not hard of hearing, and neither is she."

"I'm just saying you may be looking for trouble where there is none. Maybe you saw it as a means to manipulate me into giving you your way."

Lisa jumped to her feet. "Are you calling me a liar?"

Michael shook his head and heaved a tired sigh. This conversation wasn't progressing at all as he had hoped. "No. I'm just not sure what this has to do with anything. If you don't like the girls, you simply avoid them."

"Mike," Josie said, "that might not be as easy as you think."

"What's hard about finding new friends?"

"Finding new friends?" Lisa's face flushed in anger. "Are you a hundred years old, or somethin'? Don't you remember how hard that is?" She appeared ready to turn on the tears again.

Not what he needed at the moment.

"You know, this has been a stressful

night." Josie refrained from blaming him. "You two haven't accomplished anything, and I have to get up in less than five hours."

"How long have you been residing here, Lisa?" he asked.

"Residing?" Lisa rolled her eyes and threw her arms up in exasperation. "Do you always have to talk like you're a dictionary?"

Josie rose to her feet. "Okay, you two. We're all testy. How about we meet tomorrow at the diner at ten-thirty, after the breakfast rush, and try this again? I'll attempt to act as moderator."

Lisa crossed her arms. "But —"

"That's final." With a clink-clink of silver jewelry, Josie pointed toward the bedrooms. "Lisa, good night."

Without another word, Lisa marched down the hallway, her ragged-edged jeans dragging along the hardwood floor. Amazed that Josie had such control over the firebrand, he couldn't help a twinge of admiration.

Though he hated to have to go through Josie to get to Lisa, at least now he knew Lisa was safe and had a roof over her head. He should be grateful to Josie for that much.

She took three steps to the front door and held it open for him.

He stepped out onto the front porch. "By

the way, can you recommend a hotel?"

"You're not going to find the Ritz."

"I don't expect the Ritz."

"No?" She attempted a tired smile. "Go right at the end of my street. Once you hit the main road, take a left. The Comfy Inn's on the right. I know the owner. She's a fanatic about cleanliness."

Apparently, Josie was starting to know him as well as she knew Lisa. "Sounds perfect." He put his hands in his pockets and inspected his shoes. "I'm sorry about tonight."

She shrugged. "No harm done to me. You ought to be apologizing to your niece."

"I'll try. If she'll even listen."

Josie gave a quiet laugh. "We'll find out, won't we?"

"I also owe you a debt of gratitude. For taking care of Lisa. I've worried where she might be resid—" He glanced across the room where she had disappeared. ". . . Where she might be staying."

Josie smiled, and he sucked in a breath. This time her smile seemed genuine, not nervous or forced. And it really packed a punch.

"You're welcome, Mike. I view it as part of my calling."

"Your calling?"

"From God. To care for people like Jesus did."

It was one thing to attend church regularly. Michael, himself, did that. But hearing God call you to take in runaways? "I see. Well, good night."

As he drove past the row of tiny wood and stone houses, he pondered his options. Not only did he have to fight a teen who hated him, but he also had to deal with a woman who, because of a calling from God, might try to come between him and that teenager.

He wondered which one would prove the more worthy adversary.

He suspected the pink-haired waitress.

CHAPTER THREE

Josie crouched behind the counter restocking the to-go boxes and paper cups. The bell on the front door clanged as someone entered. It was almost time for Mike to arrive, and her pulse kicked up a notch.

She hurriedly stacked the items and wadded up the plastic they came in. By the time she finished, a hint of Mike's rich, enticing aftershave had wafted her way.

It's definitely him.

Was she forever destined to be stooped behind the counter when he arrived? Her nose would know him better than her eyeballs would.

She stood up, smoothed the wrinkles out of her uniform and found him in the same corner booth he'd sat in yesterday. She could have guessed he would be a creature of habit. "Mornin', Mike. How'd you sleep?"

When he looked up at her, she wanted to

groan. The morning sunlight streamed in through the window she had cleaned earlier. It reflected off his shiny black hair. The blue of his eyes was so deep it appeared blue-violet. Thick, dark lashes made her want to shout that it wasn't fair.

The creature was even more spectacular in daylight.

He scanned the grill area. "My niece better be here."

The suspicion in those intense eyes snapped her right back to reality. He might be beautiful, but he wasn't someone she should be thinking about that way.

"I asked you how you slept last night," she said. "Shouldn't you answer before you start barking orders?"

One eyebrow lifted ever so slightly, and she thought for a second his mouth would follow suit. "I slept fairly well, thank you."

"So everything was up to snuff?"

"The accommodations were fine. I appreciate the recommendation."

"Good. I'll run and get Lisa from the back. She's washing pots and pans."

"Bud hired her?"

"Sort of. He pays her a little. But mostly, she's here to help me. She gets a cut of the tips. And room and board."

"I'll certainly reimburse you for any lodging and food."

Yet another reason to ignore his gorgeous eyes and yummy smell. Everything had a price for men like him. She waved off his offer and went to holler through the kitchen door for Lisa. Then she returned and slid into the booth across from him. Fiddling with her bracelets, she tried to look anywhere but at those amazing eyes.

"You like jewelry, I see," he said.

"It's one of my weaknesses. I don't shop for clothes or shoes. But get me in a bead shop, and I go crazy."

"Do you mean you make the pieces yourself?"

"Most of them. It's relaxing."

"I don't think I've ever met anyone who made her own jewelry."

At the tone of his voice, a burst of irritation flared through her chest and right out her mouth. "Well, I can't quite afford to shop at Tiffany's."

"I didn't mean —"

Lisa plopped in the booth beside Josie and said, "I'm not gonna, like, jump when you say jump or anything. But I promised Josie I'd listen."

Wishing he could take back his careless comment about the jewelry, Michael refocused his attention on the problem at hand.

"I want to apologize about last night, Lisa. I know it scared you."

"Forget it. It doesn't matter."

"Well, I want you to know I'm sorry."

"I said forget it, okay?" Lisa practically shouted.

Stunned by her vehemence, he gave Josie a look that asked, *What now?*

"Okaaay . . ." Josie rubbed her hands together. "Now that that's out of the way, let's see if we can get you two to come to some kind of agreement about what Lisa is going to do. The rules are no shouting, or Bud'll kick you out. No name-calling and bad-mouthing each other, or *I'll* kick you out. Agreed?"

"Agreed," Michael said and waited for his niece to say the same.

Instead, she crossed her arms protectively in front of herself, her chin almost touching her chest.

"Lisa?" Josie said.

"Mmm."

The sound could mean anything, but Michael assumed it was acquiescence.

"Good," Josie said. "Now, Michael, tell Lisa why you're here."

"I think that's fairly obvious. I came to find her."

Josie nodded toward his niece. "Tell Lisa,

not me."

He sighed, but leaned his arms on the table and looked at the top of her green head. "Lisa, I was worried about you. I want you to agree to come home with me."

In one quick motion Lisa's whole demeanor changed. She sat straight up, eyes on him. "Do you mean it, Uncle Michael? You really want me to come home with you?"

The expectant look on her face nearly undid him. He would have to explain his plans carefully. "Home to Charleston. You need the supervision and care they give you at school. Come back, and I'll talk to the headmistress about changing the expulsion to a suspension, about letting you make up your missed work. I'm sure she can . . ."

As he watched, the life seemed to drain back out of Lisa. *What do I do now?* He looked to Josie, who rubbed her forehead as if he'd given her a headache. "Surely you both understand," he said.

"Understand, nothin'," Lisa said. "Just go on back to the bank. I'm fine here."

"But you belong in Charleston with us. With your family," he said.

"Yeah, well, I'm sure you'll get along without me."

"Mike, why don't you tell Lisa why you

want to send her back to boarding school," Josie suggested.

"Everyone needs a good education. You're getting the best money can buy."

Josie winced. "Tell Lisa why you worry. Why you want her somewhere safe."

He watched as Lisa slunk a little lower in the booth. Another inch or two and she'd slither onto the floor.

Somehow, the pitiful green hair and slight frame made her seem vulnerable. His heart lurched. No matter how you dressed her up — fingernail polish, hair color, body piercings — she still looked just like her mother.

"I worry about boys taking advantage," he blurted. "I worry about you being on your own at sixteen. It's my responsibility to keep you safe."

"It sounds like Mike is scared you'll have some of the same problems your mother had," Josie said. She searched for confirmation.

He nodded.

"I don't want to talk about my mother."

"Even though I wasn't able to help her, maybe I can help you," Mike said.

"I'm not going to talk about her."

Silence.

"Okay, Lisa," Josie said. "Can you try to tell your uncle how you feel?"

She shook her head no.

"Come on, tell him some of the things you've told me."

"Won't make a difference."

"I do care, Lisa," Michael said.

"Big whoop."

"I really do."

"Then prove it," Lisa said.

"Okay. How can I prove it to you?"

"Take me home. *Home.* Not to that snob factory."

She stared directly at him. A spark of something — challenge? — lit her blue eyes, but then it was gone. Couldn't she see that he wasn't suitable? That he couldn't possibly take care of a teenage girl?

Lisa jumped up and stalked toward the kitchen. "Yeah, I see how much you care."

He tried to hustle out of the booth, but flinched in pain as his knees struck the underside of the too-small table. "Lisa, wait."

"Whatever," she called back over her shoulder.

Standing by the grill watching the scene, Bud frowned. Michael raced past him and stormed through the kitchen door with Josie close on his heels.

"Stop right there, young lady," he said.

"Uh-huh. And what are you going to do if

I don't?"

"I'll, I'll . . ."

Josie approached and put an arm around Lisa's shoulders. "Come on, let's go try to talk some more."

Lisa shook off Josie's arm. "I'm outta here."

As his niece rushed out the back door, Michael thought he saw tears on her cheeks. He looked at Josie, who stood there looking at him, shaking her head as if he'd blown everything.

He threw his arms out. "What?"

"Is this how it always goes with you two?"

"I tried. I don't seem to be good at relating to Lisa."

"That's an understatement."

"Thanks for the vote of confidence."

"You've got a lot to learn about this parenting business, Mike."

He glared at her. "And I suppose you think you'd be a great parent?"

"Well, you have to admit I'm doing a little better with your niece."

"Only because you don't have to be the bad guy. Try sending her back to school where she belongs and see how long you stay her hero."

"Where she belongs? Does she belong separated from everyone she loves?"

He reeled from the unexpected barb. "Fine. Maybe I should simply wash my hands of this mess and get back to running my business."

"That's not a bad idea. She could live with me for a while, and I can get her enrolled in the local high school."

The worst part was that Josie probably *could* get Lisa to go to school when he couldn't even manage to have a normal conversation with her. Which infuriated him. "No Throckmorton's going to mooch off a stranger. She'll finish school where I put her."

Josie shook her head and looked away as if she couldn't stand the sight of him. "I've gotta get back to my shift. I'll find Lisa when I get off at two o'clock to make sure she's okay." Josie pushed back through the door to the diner.

Michael walked in a circle, so furious at his ineptitude that he started to kick the refrigerator. But he stopped right before his foot connected with the stainless steel industrial-sized appliance. It would most likely win the match. And he wouldn't feel any better anyway.

Mortified at his outburst, he checked the back of his shirt to make sure it was still neatly tucked in.

No, he wouldn't feel any better. Not until he got out of this tourist trap town, with Lisa in tow, and back to the bank.

When Josie left the diner after her shift, she shielded her eyes from the bright sun, then took a deep breath of fresh air. When she got to her car, she found Mike leaning against the driver's side door.

He held up one hand to stop her. "Before you chastise me, let me say I'm here to try to make amends for how poorly I handled this morning."

The anger she'd fed all afternoon vanished. He stood with ankles crossed, arms folded in front of himself — he in his designer-brand clothes against her clunker car. She grinned. "I can't imagine a more mismatched pair than you and Betty."

"Betty?"

"My car."

"So you're one of *those* people." He smiled.

"You got it. Betty and I, we're pretty attached to each other."

"Then maybe Betty would like to meet Jeffery sometime."

Her mouth fell open. "No way. Not you."

"Yes, ma'am. I repeatedly refused my parents' offer of a driver. Finally told them

I already had Jeffery. They never asked again."

Trying to picture him doing something so whimsical, she burst out laughing. Then again, for him, it had been practical. "Just when I think I have you all figured out . . ."

He opened her door for her.

She searched the street, but didn't see his car. "Did you walk here?"

"Yes. Thought I could use the time to think."

She squeezed past him and slipped into her split, vinyl car seat. "So why are you here?"

"I thought I'd offer to help check on Lisa."

Josie considered his offer for a few seconds. "Can you manage not to upset her again?"

One side of his mouth quirked up. "I doubt it."

That was for certain. They were like oil and water. "Oh, all right, get in."

As Michael climbed in, he thanked God that Josie was willing to help out with Lisa. He'd replayed the morning's scene over and over in his mind since he'd left the diner.

"You know where you went wrong this morning, Mike?"

He watched her profile as she drove. "Are you a mind reader?"

"No. Just assuming you're here because you feel guilty."

"I never should have used the word *home* synonymously with school."

"Bingo."

"Contrary to what you might think, I do learn from my mistakes."

She sucked in her breath. "You? Mistakes?"

With a smile, he faced the road again. "Never. Just lapses in judgment."

"I see. Well, I suggest you tread carefully from here on out. Remember, Lisa is an injured girl who craves a family who loves her and wants her."

Michael's heart and stomach hurt simultaneously. *How could I forget?* "You know, taking care of a teenager is quite an undertaking even for family. Doing so just because you were a runaway yourself doesn't make much sense."

"Oh, it's more than that. I told you, it's my calling. To help people like Jesus would."

"How did you discover your calling?"

"After I settled here in Gatlinburg, I realized that I didn't really have a purpose in my life. So I asked God to give me one."

"And he sent you Lisa?"

"Yes. But he sent a few other girls first, through a ministry at my church."

"What happened with them?"

She slowed to a stop behind a line of traffic. "Are you sure you want to know?"

He wasn't sure at all. "I should probably know your track record."

"Two have gone home, reunited with their families. One, Regina, is living on her own here in town and attending the community college. Another couldn't get off drugs and ran off when I got tough with her."

"At least you tried."

She smiled at him. "Thank you for saying that. I still worry about her."

They pulled up to the craft school, and this time she let Michael go all the way up to the campus with her. They stepped out of the car and into what looked like an art gallery and found doors leading to, presumably, studios. Josie seemed to know where she was going.

"Have you been here before?" he asked.

"Yes, I took a jewelry making class a couple of years ago."

"Impressive."

"Lower your brows a notch. You don't have to look so surprised."

"I'm not at all surprised. Your passion for what interests you is to be admired."

Color flooded her cheeks, and he had a powerful urge to run his thumbs over their

71

warmth.

Instead, he clenched his hands. "Let's find Lisa."

"I have a feeling she's in there." She pointed to a door marked Fibers, peeked in, then motioned him over.

He looked over the top of Josie's head, the wild bits of hair tickling his chin. She smelled like the diner, which made his empty stomach rumble. But her hair also held the faint aroma of peaches. *Intriguing.* He would have expected something sassy, something spicy.

Lisa, deep in conversation with a guy working at a large loom, didn't see them. Josie backed into Michael, pushing him out of the way, so she could quietly close the door.

"Has she come to watch that artisan before?"

"Yes, and anyone else who has a talent that interests her."

"You mean she's truly interested in art?"

Josie cocked her head to the side and gave him a smile just short of friendly. "Shouldn't you know?"

She was right. And he didn't like it at all. It seemed that he, who was so proficient at work, was failing more and more on a personal level. Most recently at his engagement to Gloria. But with far more devastating consequences, he'd failed at protecting his sister.

Now here he was, a dismal failure at guardianship. He didn't even know what kinds of things Lisa liked — other than outrageous hair color.

"Come on," he said. "Let's leave before she sees us."

As Josie and Mike sat in silence, stuck in traffic on the main drag, Josie prayed for Lisa and her uncle. It was as plain as an egg over-easy that Lisa craved his love and attention. But he was clueless. Clueless of her needs. Clueless about what to do to meet those needs.

Lord Jesus, give me wisdom. Help me know what to do to help the two of them. It seems that somehow, I could teach them how to relate. How to — "That's it!"

"What?" Mike asked.

She pulled into the parking lot at the Comfy Inn and stopped next to Mike's Beemer. "I have an idea."

"Is that a good thing?" The skeptical look on his face was almost comical. And he couldn't seem to get out of the car fast enough.

He came around to her window, and she

grabbed the duct-taped window crank. After she spent an exhausting thirty seconds rolling it down, he said, "I guess I should ask what it is."

"Look, Mike. I have a suggestion. An offer, really."

"Okay." There was that skeptical look again.

"Lisa needs you. And you need to get to know Lisa so you can be a better parent."

"Guardian."

"Parent. What's so hard about admitting that you're more than an uncle now?"

"You said you had an offer?"

"How about you plan to hang around for several days. I'll try to get a few afternoons off to help you get to know your niece."

"And what do I owe you in return?"

"Don't start grabbing your wallet. I just want to help."

"Like Jesus did."

"Exactly!" She laughed with the sheer joy of finally getting a point across to him. But then she noticed his hands in his pockets and that he was studying his feet. "You don't believe in God, do you?" she asked.

Though Michael was surprised she'd drawn such a conclusion, he immediately began to wonder about practicalities, such as how he would stay away from the bank for several more days. "Oh, I believe. I'm a Christian. It's just that . . . well . . ." He checked his watch.

"Oooh," she growled. "I forgot. You don't have *time* for your niece." She slung her arms in the air, setting off an alarm of jangling bracelets. "You're hopeless, Mike."

She backed up the car and squealed out of the motel lot. All because he'd looked at his watch.

Well, he couldn't help that he had responsibilities. He had stockholders depending on him. And his family's good name.

And Lisa, his conscience tried to tell him. He pushed the thought aside as he fumbled with the key to his room. When he finally unlocked the door, he stormed in and kicked the door shut behind him. He would check in with his brother at the office to see how the Mason account was going. Then he would know how much time he had left to persuade Lisa to go back to the boarding school.

He reached his secretary who put him through to Gary's secretary. Finally, his brother picked up. "Hello, Michael. How's Lisa?"

"She's fine. Just not too happy to see me."

Gary chuckled. "Did you really think she'd make it easy on you?"

With a deep sigh, and feeling older than his thirty-two years, he collapsed into a chair. "Do you think you and Dad could spare me for a couple more days? She's refusing to come home."

"I'd be glad to. You've got more important matters to take care of."

Maybe Josie was right — he was hopeless. Because he would rather be dealing with fluctuating interest rates than with the fluctuating hormones of a teenager.

"So, are you managing okay?" Michael asked. There was a pause, and he began to fear the worst.

"To tell you the truth, I've never been happier."

Happy? Michael had been challenged, fulfilled — and lately, suffocated — by the job. But it had been a while since he could claim he was happy. Probably not since the first year or two when he'd had his dad's full attention and approval.

"Sounds like you're handling things nicely, Gary. Just be sure to call me if Tom Mason needs anything. I think he'll do his financing with us this time, then we'll aim for the umbrella of all their business."

"I promise, I won't let you down big brother," Gary said before he hung up.

Michael had a perfectly capable brother

who didn't need him. And a perfectly rebellious niece who did.

He clasped his hands behind his head.

Dear God, I know I haven't spent enough time in prayer lately. I've felt cold inside since Patricia died and left me with Lisa to care for. Please give me guidance. I'm not used to having a living, breathing creature depending on me — not beyond a paycheck, anyway. Now Josie's made this offer to help me get to know Lisa.

With interlocked fingers, he massaged the back of his neck where a dull throb pounded out the beat of his heart.

It galled him to think he could need the help of the infuriating woman. Who was she to tell him how to do anything? Why, he could buy —

He stopped, a sick ache gnawing at him.

Forgive me, Lord, for the sin of pride.

If he could only find some way to persuade Lisa to leave Gatlinburg, then he wouldn't have to depend on Josie. *God, help me do this Your way, not my own.*

The shrill ring of the ancient motel phone jerked his head up. He stared at the rotary dial a moment, perplexed, as if God Himself were calling. Then he laughed at the ridiculousness of the notion and answered it. "Hello?"

"I'm sorry I told you you're hopeless."

Stunned to hear Josie on the line, he didn't respond.

"I felt guilty all the way home. And I can't concentrate on anything."

He waited, a smile creeping up on him, to see how apologetic Josie could be.

"Mike, are you there?"

Amazingly, the sound of her voice cheered him, and something warm released inside him. "You're having a nice conversation all by yourself."

"Why, you smart-aleck, good-for-nothing —"

"I thought you were calling to be nice."

She made that funny little growling sound again. The one she made when she got aggravated. "Look, I'm sorry, okay? God has been convicting me like crazy. I'm convinced He's been urging me to call you. So here I am."

The hairs on his arms prickled with chill bumps. "So what now?"

"My offer still stands. I'm willing to help you."

"If you really wanted to help me, you'd talk Lisa into going home."

"Not until you prove to me you'll be a good father to that love-starved girl."

Love-starved? A good father? It was enough

to send him running the other direction.

But he had just asked God for guidance. Maybe He was providing it through Josie.

"Deal," he said before he talked himself out of it.

"Deal?"

"Yes. You just promised to talk Lisa into going home with me if I learn to be a good . . . father."

She remained silent.

"Josie?"

She sighed. "Okay. I'll do it."

He knew he'd accepted a deal she hadn't meant to make. But despite the short time he'd known her, he was certain she would keep her word. Now he better understood why Lisa trusted Josie.

Out of the blue, his sister's face flashed though his mind, jarring him to think rationally. He'd just agreed to learn to be a guardian, a protector — a father — to his niece.

He'd just agreed to the impossible.

CHAPTER FOUR

Josie set a box of beads and tools on the end table, then grabbed her mug and inhaled the rich aroma of coffee. She exhaled all the stress of the day. After a tense twenty-four hours, she deserved this break, a chance to make a pair of earrings she'd recently designed.

As she curled up on the couch in her oldest sweatpants and sweatshirt, wet hair wrapped in a towel, satisfaction washed over her like the hot shower she'd just finished.

I've done what God asked me to do for Mike and Lisa. Nothing feels better.

Of course, she had no idea what the next step would be. But for now, all was well in the Miller household. She could enjoy the rest of her afternoon off and —

The doorbell rang. She was going to have to kill Lisa. "I'm coming," she yelled, then groaned as she climbed out of her comfortable cocoon. So much for a peaceful afternoon.

She opened the door. "Lisa, if you forgot your key, I'm —"

Mike stood on the doorstep. "Looks like I interrupted."

She held up her coffee mug. "Only the first relaxing moment I've had for myself in a week."

"Oh. No big deal, then."

"No big deal?" *You big selfish jerk.*

He smiled. A dangerous smile that sent her insides into a tailspin.

"Seriously, I'm sorry," he said. "I should have called first."

With a confused tug on her sweatshirt, she said, "Well, yeah. And remember it next time."

He laughed. "You shouldn't take life so seriously all the time. There is such a thing as kidding."

"Don't talk to me about being serious. Take a look in the mirror."

"I'm the one who dropped by spontaneously, aren't I?"

"You know, Mike, I never know what to expect from you." She stepped back from the door. "Come on in. I guess you're here to see Lisa."

"I am. I thought we could start getting to

know each other by having dinner out."

"Good idea. But she's not here yet."

"She's still at the studio with that artist?"

"I assume so."

His eyes narrowed. "Shouldn't she be supervised?"

"She's too old for me or you to be following her around."

"I guess I do need to give her some room."

"Room to make mistakes. To live and learn."

After he sat on the couch, he spread his big hands over his knees. "I plan to help her avoid the mistakes her mother made."

"Maybe your sister wouldn't have made the big mistakes if she'd been allowed to make smaller ones along the way."

Instead of replying, he leaned his forearms on his thighs and studied the floor as if it might hold the answer to all his problems.

Josie left him to his thoughts and went to remove the towel from her hair and to grab the hairbrush from the bathroom counter. She returned and plopped down in her favorite chair — the one that was so well worn she had trouble getting out of it sometimes. "I have no idea how your sister was raised. It's just something to think about."

"You may be right. We were all overprotective."

As she brushed the tangles out of her matted hair, she watched the emotions play across Mike's face. "I take it she was rebellious."

"Always."

"Did your parents pressure her to fit their mold? Like they're pressuring Lisa?"

He thought for a minute. "No. But all three of us were expected to act like . . . well, Throckmortons."

"Yep. Just like me."

"Your parents expected you to act like a Throckmorton?" His mouth twitched in a near-smile, but he still looked sad.

She grinned back. "No, I didn't have to reach such lofty ideals. I only had to be a mere Miller."

"Ah. I see."

"You know, you'd probably be surprised at how much your sister and I would have had in common."

"But you turned out fine." He shrugged. "Obviously, she didn't."

"So it's been about a year since she died?"

"Yes."

Her curiosity — and intuition — made her ask, "Were there unusual circumstances surrounding her death?"

"Besides driving drunk at ninety miles per hour and careening off the road?" His tone cut off further questioning. It made Josie wonder exactly what had happened. Then again, maybe he'd simply never grieved and didn't want to face it now.

She would drop the subject since he seemed so determined. "So, do you want to take Lisa out by yourself tonight?" she asked.

"I had planned on it." His eyes widened when he finally quit studying the floorboards and noticed Josie brushing her hair. His mother had probably taught him it was all kinds of rude for a woman to brush her hair in front of a man. Josie's own mother would pitch a fit.

"I'd love a nice quiet evening at home," Josie said. "But it might not be best for Lisa."

"In other words, she'll probably refuse to go with me."

"I didn't say that. Not exactly." Josie laughed. "Where were you planning to take her?"

"Somewhere nice so we can talk."

"As your official adviser . . . forget it."

"I'm not taking her to a fast-food joint."

"A fast-food place would be perfect." She pointed her hairbrush at him. "Remember, she's not a client you're trying to impress."

"Give me a *little* credit."

Josie pushed her way out of the chair. "Let's go find Lisa. It'll just take me a sec to fix my hair."

As she fought a stubborn tangle, he nodded toward her head. "It's a fairly normal color when it's wet."

She stopped mid tug. "You would never say that to anyone else."

"Since I've been here, I've surprised myself a few times."

She had sensed subtle changes in him already. "Hey, no problem. I think a person should speak his mind."

"Okay, then. Why's it pink?"

That was Lisa's story to tell. "Let's just say it was a disastrous adventure."

"Then why haven't you gone to a salon to have it corrected?"

Because that would make a dent in my savings. "I'm cheap." She shrugged. "And I figure my pink with Lisa's green brightens up the diner."

Michael sat in the fast-food restaurant's indoor play area across from Lisa and Josie. The artificial light turned their hair hideous colors, which did nothing to brighten up *this* dining establishment.

And this wasn't just any establishment. Lisa, who'd insisted Josie come along, had also insisted they drive until they found one that had an indoor playground. They'd passed two perfectly good hamburger places. Now he knew why.

She'd chosen a table in the massive, echoing chamber on purpose. The decibel level, hitting around one-fifty as a child got his toe stepped on, prohibited any conversation at all.

So much for starting off with a nice bonding experience.

Concern swept over him as he watched his niece merely pick at the kid's meal she'd ordered. She'd eaten about three fries and one bite of cheeseburger. She'd ingested more ketchup than anything else.

"You need to eat more than that, Lisa," he hollered.

"I'll get fat."

He nodded toward Josie. "She's eaten every bite of a combo meal and isn't fat."

Josie huffed. "Thanks for telling everyone for miles around."

Pointing to the plastic tubes filled with kids, he raised his voice another notch. "If Lisa hadn't placed us in the middle of this cacophony just to avoid talking to me, I wouldn't have to yell."

86

Josie sighed. He could see it, anyway. Not hear it. And she barely shook her head.

He'd blown it again. Why couldn't he think before criticizing? It obviously didn't do an ounce of good. As he watched in dread, Lisa slammed her uneaten food back into the word-search-decorated sack and dumped it — with great show — into the trash bin before stalking out of the restaurant.

He followed her lead and threw away the last couple of bites of his chicken sandwich. "I guess we're leaving."

"Okay by me." Josie cleaned her mess off the table.

As they exited the play area, and he could once again hear himself think, he said, "Does Lisa always eat so poorly?"

"I've had to remind her to eat sometimes, especially breakfast. But she seemed to eat okay before —"

He waited a moment, then filled in the blank. "Before I arrived."

"I'm sorry. But, yes. This was the worst she's eaten since I met her."

"I guess it'll just take time."

"Yeah. Don't worry about it. And don't pressure her."

Easier said than done.

Once he and Josie filed into his car, joining Lisa, and buckled seat belts, he adjusted his rearview mirror to see his niece in the backseat. "I'm sorry, Lisa. I have no right to comment on what you eat or on your choice of restaurant. You're old enough to make those decisions."

In his peripheral vision, Josie smiled. "See, Lisa. He's teachable. And that's exactly what we're going to do."

"Whadaya mean?" she asked.

This was the moment he'd avoided all evening. Lisa wouldn't be happy when she heard about the deal he and Josie had made. "She means . . . well, that I'm going to stay in town for a few days while she helps me learn to be a good . . . guardian."

"You're teaming up against me?"

"No," they said together.

"He —"

"She —" they said at the same time.

"See, you're giving me the company line already," Lisa said.

Josie turned around in her seat. "Lisa, honey, your uncle needs to learn what you're all about. I offered to help."

Lisa looked out the car window, her arms crossed tightly in front of herself. "If you two gang up on me, I'm out the door."

"I promise we won't," Michael said. "Just promise me you'll give it a chance."

"I'm not promising anything."

Would she promise if he threatened to lock her in the car until she did? Michael wanted to yell in frustration. His hands shook as he started the car and put it in Reverse. He didn't trust himself to speak. Nice words, words of assurance, weren't possible at the moment.

Please, God, help me understand how her mind works. Give me patience when all I want to do is shake her and make her do exactly what I want her to do. Why can't she see that I want what is best for her?

He swallowed hard to block the lump of fear trying to work its way to the surface.

Even with the dinner debacle, Michael managed to sleep that night. He awakened to a gorgeous morning in the Smoky Mountains and sipped coffee while standing on the surprisingly generous balcony of his motel room overlooking the Little Pigeon River. Crystal-clear water rushed over mounds of smooth, mossy rocks, creating a constant roar. The sound had lulled him to sleep at 10:00 p.m., the first time he'd been to bed before midnight in years.

Now, with caffeine fix in hand, he was more prepared to take on the world. Lisa included.

But first, he needed to call home. He dialed his parents' house.

"Hello?" his dad said.

"Hi. It's me."

"Are you and Lisa coming home today?"

"No, sir. It's going to take some work to make her come along with me."

"Well — Hold on, you mother's saying something." He put his hand over the phone, muffling the sound, then removed it. "Your mother says to tell Lisa to call her. She wants to talk with her."

Which meant that Grandmother wanted to lecture Lisa, trying to list all the reasons she needed to return to Charleston. He could just picture Josie's reaction to his mother's newest demands. "Tell Mother that we'll be there as soon as we possibly can."

"Michael, I expect you back at the bank to tie up the Mason account."

"I'm in touch with Gary on that. He can handle it."

"I'm not so sure. We need you back here."

"As soon as I'm finished dealing with Lisa."

"You can't reason with the child. Bring her back whether she wants to come or not."

Up until last night, he would have been inclined to agree that would be the best way to handle the situation. Now, he knew better, but he wouldn't be able to convince his dad.

"I'm sorry, Michael, your mother is signaling that we've got to hurry to be on time for Sunday school."

"I'm so off schedule, I had forgotten today was Sunday." And he hadn't thought to make plans with Josie and Lisa.

He ended the call and donned the one suit he'd packed back when he'd had hope of making Saturday's dinner meeting — the dinner he'd planned to have with Tom Mason at Magnolia's. The one he'd missed while eating surrounded by shrieking kids.

At least Gary, who'd filled in for the engagement, had gotten to enjoy the shellfish and grits.

As he dialed Josie's phone number, he hesitated. Would they welcome him to attend church with them? Would Josie even insist that Lisa go?

The phone rang.

" 'Lo?" a froggy voice croaked.

"Good morning."

Josie cleared her throat. "Mike?"

"I'm calling to invite myself to church."

"Church? What time is it?"

"It's ten o'clock. I wasn't sure what time the service would start."

She groaned. "Oh, no. We overslept."

"Does worship start at eleven?"

"Yes."

"If you don't mind, I'd like to join you and Lisa this morning."

"It was pretty rough last week when I forced her to go. It won't be easy, especially with you in the picture."

"I'm willing to try."

She sighed, and he heard sheets rustling. "Okay. We'll be ready in a flash."

As Josie and Lisa hustled out of the house, Mike opened the car door for his niece. Josie could tell by his wide-eyed look that Lisa's black dress, black boots, multiple metal belts and black lipstick horrified him. Lisa's pleased smile, and the devious sparkle in her eye, fairly shouted her victory. But Mike's determined glint as he opened Josie's door said that Lisa hadn't yet won this war.

Both confirmed that Josie was dealing with some major stubborn genes here.

Mike hopped in his side. "Where to?"

"Not that mausoleum we went to last week," Lisa said.

"That's not nice, Lisa," Mike said, though Josie understood why Lisa would say it.

"I didn't fit in at all there. The average

age must be ninety."

Josie laughed. "More like seventy. But I know a few teenagers, one who lived with me for a while. I'll introduce you this time."

"Which way, then?" Mike asked as he started his car. "Is it that big church I saw up on the hill in town?"

The one that looked exactly like the church Josie had grown up in? No, thanks. "No. It's much smaller. A little less threatening to me."

"How can a church be threatening?"

"I don't do huge crowds, okay?"

"Okay. So, left or right at the end of your street?"

Lisa leaned forward, placing her black-clad arms over the seat between them. "If we don't go soon, I'm getting out. I have lunch plans with Brian this afternoon."

"Go left," Josie said as Mike backed away from the house.

With a tug on his suit coat, Mike turned and put the car in Drive. "How about we spend the day together since neither of you is scheduled to work?"

"How about . . . no. I said I have a date."

Tension radiated off Mike's stiff shoulders. Broad shoulders that filled out the eight or nine hundred dollar suit coat to perfection.

"What do you know about him, Lisa? Is he a Christian?"

"Like I'm going to ask that on the first date."

"You need to know that about all potential boyfriends."

"Look, he goes to church with his family every time the doors open. Does that satisfy you?"

"Josie, what do you think about this Brian guy?"

"He's always been responsible delivering the bread. On time. Professional. Polite."

Mike stopped at an intersection, and she directed him to turn. As he rested his arm on the back of the seat to look around at his niece, the exotic, masculine smell of his aftershave lotion wafted her way. Josie sniffed the scent of spice and man deep into her lungs and somehow managed not to nuzzle against his large, hair-dusted hand. What was wrong with her?

"I guess if Josie thinks he's okay, you can go out with him," Mike said to Lisa.

Josie couldn't believe her ears. He actually trusted her judgment?

"But don't think you're going to use him as an excuse every time we plan an activity," he added.

"You're not going to plan every minute of

every day, Uncle Michael. I have a life, you know."

"You have a life at school. This is more like a vacation, and you should be thankful I'm allowing you to stay."

Once the car was moving again, Lisa started muttering in the backseat. Josie wasn't sure Michael could hear, but she heard loud and clear as Lisa griped about him being bossy.

As they pulled into the lot of the stone church near the diner, she noticed Michael's tanned knuckles had turned white as his fingers gripped the steering wheel.

Apparently, he had heard after all.

"We're here," he said.

This was her church, her sanctuary when she had come to town, hurting, disillusioned, alone. She'd met a kind, older woman who owned the Comfy Inn. Susan had taken Josie under her wing and eventually invited her to visit a service. Josie hadn't missed a Sunday since.

A couple of teenagers walked through the parking lot. And a family with a baby.

"See, Lisa, two kids your age," Mike pointed out.

A smart-alecky huffing sound was her only response.

Josie wondered if it was due to the fact

that the teens, a boy and a girl, were dressed very conservatively or the fact that they were actually a couple, holding hands.

Maybe Regina would be there. Lisa could relate to another runaway.

The instant they came to a complete stop in a parking space, Lisa climbed out and slammed the door. Josie reached for Mike and peeled first one finger, then the next out of the death grip. "Relax," she said near his ear. "Don't let her goad you. You play right into her hands."

He straightened his fingers, wiggled them a second, then turned the car off and removed the keys. As he leaned to his side and dropped them into his pocket, he looked her in the eye. "Thank you."

Unable to resist touching him, she took his hand and squeezed. She was a compassionate person, after all. And he seemed to be working so hard. How could she not like a guy who kept trying to win over a girl who loved to torment him? "Hang in there, Mike. You're doing better already."

"Yeah? How's that?"

"You didn't blow up when she grumbled there in the backseat."

"Only because she was trying to talk to herself. She just needed to let off some steam."

Josie laughed and opened her door. "I'm sure we all need to pray for patience while we're here."

Josie sure had the part about praying for patience right, Michael thought as he slipped into the second pew from the front — thanks to Josie who insisted that if they were going to worship, then they needed to sit close to the choir.

He also needed to do some repenting because his thoughts hadn't been exactly pure as Josie had studied his hands, had whispered in his ear, had touched him. He could have sworn he'd even seen her inhale when she was close to him, as if she enjoyed the smell of his aftershave lotion.

Heavenly God, direct my thoughts. Keep them focused on You. Keep them on my mission here. I may not understand Your plan for me, how Lisa plays into that, but I know Josie's face shouldn't keep intruding in my thoughts. . . .

The friendly congregation settled in. Lisa, with her arms crossed in their usual position, sat between him and Josie. As Josie put her arm around Lisa and whispered something in her ear, Josie's fingertips rested on his shoulder. When the pastor welcomed everyone, drawing her attention away, her fingers remained, warming him through the wool.

Her mere fingertips had the power to send his train of thought awry. How could this unusual woman affect him so? Gloria had never given him a moment of trouble. She was calm, controlled, dignified. He'd never worried what she might say or do. She knew exactly what to do in every situation.

Then again, Josie seemed to know what to do in every situation as well. So what was the difference? Why did he find her so disturbing?

He picked up the hymnal as they sang the opening hymn. Along about the second verse, he caught movement out of the corner of his eye.

Josie seemed entranced. Her face tilted heavenward.

There was his answer right there. He found her disturbing because she was so unpredictable. The woman who had talked about being intimidated by crowds had settled in the midst of this crowd as if she'd been born to it. Without a whit of self-consciousness, she sang at the top of her lungs.

Maybe that adaptability was what made it so easy for her to connect to God. To connect with Lisa.

Could she teach him how to do that? Possibly even how to love?

Whether she could or not, he needed to remember that he could never consider a relationship with someone so unpredictable. He enjoyed a planned and orderly life. Lisa would cause enough turmoil. He certainly didn't need to add the chaos that was Josie to the mix.

CHAPTER FIVE

"Wow," Josie said as they drove away from the church. "That was the most uplifting service I've ever gone to." Joy still warmed her.

Lisa leaned her chin on the back of Josie's seat. "You said that last week. And you know, Josie, it could get a little embarrassing to have you belting out songs like that."

"I couldn't help it. The joy of the music just bubbled out of me."

"That's cool, I guess. As long as it's not for show."

Michael cocked his head back in surprise. "That was a quick about-face, Lisa — from embarrassing to cool."

"Hey, as long as Josie's being honest, I can live with the wacky."

"And is your choice of Sunday clothes a statement of your honesty?" he asked.

Josie tensed, waiting for Lisa's explosion.

But Lisa chuckled. "I guess you can say

that. I honestly love black."

"As long as it's not just for show." He raised his brows at her in the rearview mirror.

She mumbled, "Yeah, well . . ."

With a smirk lifting one side of his mouth, he glanced at Josie, then said to Lisa, "Hey, you look good in black. It sets off the green nicely."

Lisa huffed. "Like you really believe that."

"I have to admit I think your natural color is more attractive. But you are sixteen and old enough to choose your own hairstyle."

Way to go, Mike. You're catching on.

"Hey, look! There's Regina, walking by the road. Slow down, Mike."

"Who's Regina?" Lisa asked.

"The girl I told you about. She lived with me for a while."

Mike pulled alongside Regina.

Josie rolled down her window. "How about a ride?"

Winded, Regina said, "That would be great. I'm late to work."

Regina climbed in the back beside Lisa, and Josie made the introductions. "Mike, let's drop Regina at the diner. She works with Bud on Sundays after church."

"I didn't see you at church," Lisa said.

"I worked in the nursery today."

101

"Oh." Lisa was silent, and Josie noticed she kept secretly checking out Regina.

"I work at the diner, too," Lisa added.

"I know. Bud talks about you and Josie all the time."

"Good things, I hope." Josie laughed, then turned around to point Mike in the right direction.

"Yes. He brags on both of you — as much bragging as Bud would do, anyway."

"Aren't you going to college somewhere nearby?" Mike asked.

"Yes, sir. I'm studying to be a social worker."

"Good for you. You'll do well, I'm sure." He pulled up in front of the diner. "Here you go."

"Did you ever go home to your parents?" Lisa blurted as Regina was getting out.

"Just to visit. I decided to stay here, to live on my own once I turned eighteen. But I talk to my parents. Everything is cool between us now."

Lisa's gaze darted to her uncle. "That's good."

"Thanks for the ride." Regina hurried to the door of the diner, then waved.

"She's nice," Lisa said. "How long did she live with you, Josie?"

"About eight months. Then she moved

out, got a roommate and applied for college."

"That sounds great."

Mike didn't look too happy about that type of plan. She smiled at him, hoping to encourage him, then turned to the backseat. "So, Lisa, what are we going to do today after your lunch date?"

"*We* aren't doing anything."

"But we need to show Mike around town. Let's do something fun after you get home."

Lisa rolled her eyes, a gesture Josie would forever associate with Lisa.

"I promise you'll enjoy yourself."

"I'm at the mercy of you ladies," Mike said. "Why don't you call when you're free this afternoon. I'll come get you, and we'll do whatever you say."

"But Brian and I —"

"Invite him along," Mike added. "I should get to know him if you're going to be socializing with him."

Lisa made a face and mouthed, "Socializing?"

Thankful that Lisa hadn't voiced her criticism and seemed to be learning, too, Josie winked at her. "We'll loosen Mike up this afternoon. Whataya say?"

"No. And Brian's supposed to pick me up at twelve-thirty, so take me home so I can change."

Mike slammed on the brakes. "Excuse me?"

Luckily no one rear-ended them.

"Take me home . . . please," Lisa uttered as if it were painful to be polite.

He started the car in motion once again and took her to Josie's house as she'd requested. But he didn't appear happy about it. Josie imagined it took all his hard-fought control not to chew her ear off the whole way.

Lisa hopped out and slammed the door. After a second of hesitation, she opened the door again. "Thank you." It was grudging, but at least she'd said it.

He watched his niece climb the front steps, take out her key and go inside. "So, what's our plan for today?" he finally asked.

"Since you're letting Lisa go out with Brian, I assumed we'd go our separate ways."

"What about showing me the town — loosening me up?"

Was the guy kidding? "That was for your and Lisa's benefit, not yours and mine."

"True. I suppose you'd like an afternoon off without us to worry about."

Was it her imagination or was he trying to send her on a guilt trip?

If so, it was working. He looked kind of lonely sitting there staring at the house.

"I guess we could get some lunch," she said, feeling sorry for him. "Why don't you go change and come back to get me?"

One side of his mouth quirked up in that way that made her stomach do somersaults. "Taking pity on me? You're not as tough as you'd like me to think."

At the moment, she was about as tough as an undercooked French fry. Just looking at him made her joints go to mush. "I'm tough when the situation calls for it. You're new to town and don't know all the good places to eat."

He nodded and pulled a face that said he didn't believe a word she'd said. "I see. So you're moonlighting at the chamber of commerce?"

"That's right." She would try to convince him even if she knew better.

"Thanks for offering, Miss Welcoming Committee. I'll go take this suit off. I should be back in time to meet this Brian fellow."

She climbed out and then tried not to look at him as he waved and drove away in all that leather and luxury.

As Josie stood wondering why she was drawn to the man, Brian drove up, ten minutes early, and honked the horn for Lisa.

She marched over to the truck. "Don't ever drive up and honk, mister. You come to the door, or you don't take her out."

He swallowed, and his overgrown Adam's apple bobbed up, then back down. "Yes, ma'am."

Before he could get out, the front door opened and Lisa barreled out. "Hey, Brian. Let's go."

"Your uncle wants to meet Brian," Josie said. "Why don't you two stick around a few minutes?"

Lisa peeked at Brian and must have noticed his horrified expression at the mention of the word *uncle*. She opened the passenger door and heaved herself into the truck. "We need to get going. Can't do it right now."

Brian appeared torn between fear and obedience.

Josie decided not to push them at the moment. "Go on, then." But she would make sure Mike and Brian met. Mike needed to see he was an okay kid, and Brian needed to see that Mike wasn't an ogre.

Josie guided Mike toward town and the many restaurants they had to choose from. She didn't suppose he would appreciate her choosing the diner.

"I still can't believe Lisa was so stubborn about not wanting the four of us to do something together today," he said.

"It's a date. Remember those?"

"Of course."

"How often did you want your parents along?"

"But she's only sixteen. What could she possibly want to do that she doesn't want me there?"

"Come on, Mike, she's not up to anything immoral or illegal. She just wants to have some fun with a boy."

He drove without further complaint, silenced by her censure. As they passed Josie's favorite miniature golf place, she spotted Brian's shiny red truck with his family's bread company logo.

Some lunch. They must've gone by a drive-through window and eaten in the truck.

"Mike, how badly do you want to prove you're a fun guy?"

He raised a skeptical eyebrow. "I'm not sure I like the sound of that."

"Lisa and Brian are over there, about to play golf."

Mike slowed and pulled into the parking lot. "I'd feel a little sneaky."

"Me, too. But we could play our own

game and hope they'll join us for a second round."

As they sat in the running car, Mike stricken with what was probably uncharacteristic indecision, Lisa and Brian rounded the corner from the little rental hut. Brian had his club and ball in his left hand and his right arm around Lisa's waist.

"Hey, he's got his hand on her rear end," Mike hollered.

"Not quite, Mike. He's just tall and has long arms." And he looked as awkward as an ape. "It's probably the first time he's had his arm around a girl."

"That's no comfort. He'll be bumbling and groping before we know it."

Lisa smiled up at Brian and appeared comfortable while Brian blushed and acted as if he didn't know what to do next. It was almost painful to watch.

Josie's conscience kicked in. They shouldn't be spying. "Maybe we should just let them be, Mike. We need to eat, anyway."

In a too-quick flash of uncoordinated movement that looked more like an attack, Brian kissed Lisa on the . . . not quite mouth, not quite cheek. As he did so, he thumped her on the head with his golf club, which knocked the golf ball out of his hand.

"What'd I tell you, Josie? Did you see that

idiotic move?"

"Yes, the poor guy. How embarrassing."

"Lisa's not pleased. She apparently doesn't want him kissing her."

Lisa walked away from him, rubbing her head. She plopped herself on a bench, threw down her club, then crossed her arms.

Before Josie could stop him, Mike turned off the car, got out and stalked up to the couple.

Poor Brian. He didn't stand a chance.

"Time to do something to salvage the day," Josie said to the empty car as she climbed out and raced after Mike.

Before he could cry uncle, Michael found himself with a fluorescent-pink golf ball in one hand and a cheap putter in the other — thanks to Josie's intervention. She'd kept him from making a scene, barely. She'd arrived just as he was about to give Brian the dressing-down of his life.

Then again, maybe Brian wasn't merely an octopus-handed coward. Maybe he was smart for hightailing it back to his truck, opting out of a friendly game of . . . Michael shielded his eyes from the sun and read the rusting sign.

Dinosaur-Putt.

For years, Michael had played golf at the

club with potential clients, but he would probably humiliate himself here in front of God, man and papier-mâché dinosaurs.

"You go first," Lisa said, anger still sparking in her voice. She wasn't happy to have had her plans ruined.

Even though she was still furious with him, she was acting more animated than she had since he'd arrived. He would gladly make a fool of himself if this was his reward.

Once he'd set the ball down, he flexed his knees, perfected his grip, gave the putter a few practice swings, then sent the ball into motion with a gentle tap.

It went about three feet.

"It must've rained last night," Josie said. "The turf's waterlogged."

He observed the moisture squishing to the surface around his shoes as he moved his weight from one foot to the other. *This is supposed to be fun?*

"Let's bend the rules. I'll let you take that one over if you want," Lisa said ever so generously. Her gleeful expression revealed that she knew just how much this was costing him in pride.

"No, I wouldn't dream of it. Who's next?"

"I am." Lisa placed her blue ball off to the side of the pad that served as a tee and gave it a whack. Right towards his ball. Blue hit pink and sent it rolling to wedge right behind a dinosaur's tail.

Does she think we're playing croquet?

"Lisa," Josie scolded. "Don't worry, Mike. You'll be able to set it one putter length away from the raptor's tail so you can hit it."

"Great."

"My turn." Josie dropped her yellow ball haphazardly, and without taking the time to line up at all gave it a firm tap. It rolled right under the dinosaur's belly, which was barely six inches off the ground, and she and Lisa rushed to watch it on the other side. As Lisa stood, arms crossed, the picture of cool, Josie leaned sideways and groaned as if trying to somehow force the ball to drop into the hole. And it did.

"Wahoo!" Josie shrieked.

"Awesome shot," said his niece.

As Josie waited for Lisa to give her a high five, she grinned at Michael. "Hole in one."

"Congratulations." *This is going to be an interminably long afternoon.*

The next two holes went pretty much the same. Josie had the luck of the Irish. Lisa didn't care what her score was as long as she got to knock Michael's ball under soggy prehistoric figures into the realm of drowned bugs.

And he bemoaned his five-over-par score.

Ever hopeful, he said, "This one has a par three, but it's a pretty straight shot. I think I can make up a stroke."

"Maybe." His niece elbowed Josie.

"Lisa, leave the poor man's ball alone so he'll have a fighting chance."

"It's what he deserves for scaring Brian away."

"Lisa . . ."

"Okay. For a while."

"Thank you for being so kind." He smiled at her, and for a moment he thought she would smile back. A real one. But what she gave him was more reserved — tilted-up mouth but no teeth showing. Still, it was a start.

Any accomplishment raised his spirits and his hope that the two of them would be heading back to Charleston soon.

The fact that he had so much further to go was sobering. But that one tilt of the mouth was enough to make him hit one under par. "Yeah," he said as he thrust his club in the air.

"Nice job, Mike. Now let's see you focus like that on the next fourteen holes." Josie wiggled her jean-clad hips as she got in place for her shot. "Maybe you'll catch up to me."

She hit another hole in one.

By the time they finished the tenth hole, he was impossibly behind Josie. But he and Lisa were neck and neck. At the moment, he was ahead by one shot. Once Lisa hit the ball, he joined the ladies as they watched the ball roll.

"Go ball, go ball, go — Yeah!" Lisa leaped in the air, then looked around as if not wanting anyone to witness a moment of excitement. "My first hole in one," she said, then pinned her lips between her teeth, trying not to grin.

Josie ruffled Lisa's hair. "Way to go."

"Congratulations, Lisa." Before he thought about what he was doing, he put his arm around her shoulders and gave her a squeeze.

She pulled away, refusing to look at him. Instead, she looked at Josie and said, "I think I'll run to the water fountain. Gotta keep this athlete hydrated."

As she rushed away, Michael's shoulders sagged. "You know, I forgot there for a moment that she wasn't ten years old."

Josie touched his arm. "She'll adjust. She's been without affection for so long. She won't even let me hug her."

Has our family done this to her, Lord? Made her afraid of human contact?

113

"Guilt's written all over you, Mike. Don't blame yourself."

"And just how do you suppose it's not my fault as much as anyone else's?"

"Did you get drunk and get yourself killed in a car wreck?"

Surprised, yet not, at her bluntness, he said, "Well, no. But maybe I did send Lisa away to school too soon. Maybe I could have called and visited more."

"I'm glad you're thinking about Lisa's welfare, Mike. But don't beat yourself up. You're here for her now."

Some of the tension eased out of him. She was right. He needed to look to the future.

He turned to the woman beside him, in her worn jeans and bright orange T-shirt. "How can a woman who's as smart as you wear orange when it clashes so badly with pink hair?"

A smile as bright as the September sun in South Carolina lit her face. "Why, thank you for noticing."

"That you clash?"

"No, silly. That I'm smart. I don't give a flip what you think about my hair."

That was the truth, for sure. He laughed as she tossed her shoulder-length hair — which she'd left down out of that bird's-nest style. Sparkly crystal-like earrings

114

caught the sun and sent flecks of rainbows across her cheek. As she went to set her ball at the next hole, he couldn't resist the attraction that raced through him. Out here in the sunshine, with regular clothes on, he didn't notice the jewelry so much as the person wearing it. She was down to earth. And likable.

Maybe too likable.

"I'm back," Lisa called. "Let's finish up."

Lisa took her place in the game, same as before, but the spark was gone. Her withdrawal from the hug made the last eight holes take forever. And the friendly competition with her dropped off as she ignored his ball. On the eighteenth hole, he actually made a hole in one to much cheering by Josie.

"Nice job, Uncle Michael." It was all Lisa said or did. No high five. No excitement.

"I'm starving. Let's go get some ice cream," Josie suggested.

Michael checked his watch. "We still need to eat lunch."

"Live on the edge, Mike. Have ice cream for lunch. You can have a regular dinner tonight."

As much as it went against his nature, he could be flexible when necessary. "Okay."

Josie punched Lisa in the arm. "What's it

going to be, sport? Your regular flavor?"

Her regular? How would Josie know that after only two weeks? He didn't even know his own mother's favorite flavor.

Lisa's mouth lifted on one side. "Yeah. What about you?"

"Since we're teaching Mike to live a little, I may as well get adventurous and try something new," Josie answered.

By the time they reached the ice-cream shop, the two women had discussed every flavor imaginable. From Apple Pie to Zippy Ripple. Whatever that was.

"I'm buying," he said.

"Of course you are. The loser always buys." Josie grinned and did that hair-flip thing again. "In fact, Lisa spent a good portion of her tips on ice cream when the two of us played last week."

He followed them to the ice-cream counter. "It looks like I've been set up."

Lisa gave him a timid half smile, her gaze darting from him to the ground. "Looks like it."

His heart almost stopped. He had an overwhelming urge to grab her and hug her to him, but it wasn't going to be possible to make up for the past year in one big bear hug. It would take a lot more work to heal her damaged spirit.

Once they ordered and found an outside picnic table, Josie sat on the bench across from him, and Lisa sat beside Josie.

"What was that concoction called again, Josie?" he asked.

"Death by Chocolate. It's got chocolate ice cream, brownies and fudge. And a little whipped cream and nuts to break the toothache-richness."

"Sounds interesting."

"Here. Take a taste." She practically shoved a bite against his lips. "Open up. It's heaven." She tapped the spoon at his tightly closed lips once more. "Come on."

He opened and the chocolate flavor burst rich and sweet on his tongue. But he dragged his gaze away from Josie to his niece. "How's the cookie dough, Lisa?"

"Good." She tentatively licked her single-scoop cone.

"What about you, Mike?" Josie leaned toward him to study his cup of ice cream.

"Vanilla."

Josie looked at Lisa and burst out laughing.

What was so funny about that?

"No way, Uncle Michael. That's against the law when there are, like, twenty-five flavors."

"It's French vanilla," he said.

"The French part doesn't count," Josie argued.

"With little flecks of vanilla bean." He tilted the cup so they could see.

Josie appraised the scoop. "Hmm, what do you think, Lisa? Is it legal if there're flecks in it?"

"That's borderline."

Josie winked at him. "It does look good."

Surely she wouldn't expect him to feed her a bite.

"Don't be stingy," she said.

He spooned up a bite and held it out to Josie. As she opened her mouth, their gazes locked. Laughter sparked in her chocolaty-brown eyes. She seemed to enjoy his discomfort with sharing food, something he considered rather intimate.

After he spooned in the portion of French vanilla, and she closed her mouth and drew away, pulling the ice cream off the spoon, she said, "Mmm. That *is* good. I never would have imagined."

He never could have imagined, either.

That evening as he dropped, exhausted, onto the motel bed, he decided it was time to reflect on his relationship with his niece.

Chocolate sauce. Sharing ice cream. The picture wouldn't leave his head.

Disgusted with his wandering mind, he forced himself to remember his goal. Proving he could take care of Lisa. And it hadn't been a bad day with her. It had been much better than the day before. She'd glowered at Brian, but he couldn't remember one time all afternoon that she had looked at him in that closed, arms-crossed position. Maybe he wasn't facing the impossible after all.

Except resisting the ridiculous attraction to Josie.

Focus, Michael.

He popped off the bed, unable to lie still. Why couldn't he quit thinking about her?

He ran his hand through his hair. *This has got to stop. It's insane.*

He jerked out his cell phone and put a call through to his brother.

Gary picked up. "Michael, it's good to hear from you. How are things —"

"How'd the dinner with Tom go?"

"What's wrong? Is Lisa —"

"She's fine. How's the Mason loan coming?"

A pause. "I wrapped it up."

"They're taking out the loan with us?"

"The loan, checking, pension, payroll . . . The whole nine yards."

What Michael had been working on for

months? The banking relationship that had eluded him? "How?"

"Tom and I connected. He said he's changed his mind and wants to work with us."

Which meant Michael had been the problem all along.

"That's great, Gary. Man . . ." He plopped down in a chair. "Congratulations. What a coup."

Gary laughed. "Does that mean you'll promote me to VP?"

"Hey, you landed the Mason accounts. You deserve it. I'll see what I can do."

"Thanks, big brother. Now, on to more important things."

Michael drew a blank. More important?

"Our niece?" Gary prompted.

Oh, of course. Lisa. His reality — at least temporary reality — so far removed from what he'd always thought was important.

But his responsibility at the bank, his place in the Charleston community . . . They didn't feel quite so much a part of him at the moment.

Then again, neither did Gatlinburg and Lisa.

Early the next morning, Josie decided it was a perfect day for a hike. As Lisa called Brian

120

to invite him, Josie tossed drinks into a cooler. Once it was full, she opened the freezer for ice.

The sight of a half gallon of French vanilla ice cream, left over from a dessert she'd made a month ago, made her smile.

"What are you grinning about?" Lisa asked as she hurried into the kitchen in baggy jeans and a Grateful Dead T-shirt.

"Oh, nothing. Just remembering something."

"Brian backed out again. Said he had to work. But I think he's afraid of Uncle Michael."

"Wouldn't you be? The man's all dark and scary whenever he mentions you and boys in the same sentence."

"He's, like, so overprotective. I'll never have a life."

"It's because he loves you and wants the best for you."

"Yeah, right."

"He does. I can tell."

"How?" Lisa acted tough, but looked so eager to hear.

As Josie racked her brain to come up with something good he'd done, she realized she didn't have to look far. Mike had improved by leaps and bounds in the three days he'd been there. "Parents have protective instincts. He's feeling what a parent feels. And that's a good thing."

"He's just afraid I'll get pregnant like my mother did."

"Yeah, well, you did run off with what's-his-name."

"I told you, we never had sex."

"How's Mike supposed to know that? Think about what it must look like to him — and to everyone else."

"The creep's long gone, so forget him."

"Your uncle's just worried about your safety. And whether you believe it or not, about your happiness."

"I know that isn't true." She slouched into a chair at the kitchen table, then twirled a salt shaker between her palms.

If only I could help her see Mike cares for her. Josie paused, then the answer hit her. "He's tried real hard not to be critical."

"Ha! It's in the Throckmorton genes to be critical."

"How so?"

"If you ever meet my grandmother, you'll know."

Josie knew about criticism from her own parents. Thinking of Lisa going through it hurt. And made her plain ol' mad. "What kinds of things does your grandmother say?"

"I'll tell you about it sometime when you

have about a week. Right now, I want us to go, to catch Uncle Michael off guard. To see if he's really human."

"Lisa, stop it. Go call to invite him."

"Wouldn't it be fun to show up without calling? To teach him to be more spontaneous?"

Josie would never admit that she was curious about the same thing. The man seemed like an automaton at times. Catching him unprepared could be a real hoot. "I guess we can surprise him if you want. But be nice."

Once they'd loaded the cooler into Betty's trunk, Josie and Lisa headed to the motel where they banged on Mike's door together. He answered it with hair standing on end, beard shadowing his face, in a T-shirt and pair of warm-up pants — barefoot.

It wasn't a hoot at all. He actually looked like someone who was her type, someone she could be interested in. The man was much more dangerous to her like this, when he didn't look rich and pulled together.

"What time is it?" he asked.

"We, uh . . . Uh. We —" Josie's mouth, or brain, wouldn't form words.

"Time to get up," Lisa said.

"What's wrong, Josie?" he asked.

Josie snapped herself out of her reverie.

He was still Mike after all. Stuffy banker. "Not a thing."

Lisa pointed at his bed-head hair. "You're a wreck. You're scaring her."

Mike reddened as he brushed his hands through his hair.

His wrinkled dress shirt from church the day before hung on the doorknob of the closet. When he yanked open the door and grabbed a pair of shoes, it fell off. After he'd slipped the shoes on, Josie handed him the shirt.

"Thanks."

Brooks Brothers shirt and Nike shoes. The fact that he wore brand-name clothes reminded her of why she shouldn't like him. Money. He wore the fact that he had loads of it like a designer label across his forehead, reminding her of all she'd run away from. Of all she refused to ever be a part of again.

And Mike's working to amass wads of the stuff had kept him from what should have been a priority: altering his busy lifestyle to keep Lisa in his home where she belonged.

Instead of giving him a lecture, Josie said, "Lisa and I came by to get you to go hiking in the national park."

He ran his hand through his hair again. A hopeful look raised his brows. "You did?"

"It was Josie's idea," Lisa blurted.

His expression fell. Josie glared a warning at Lisa. "Actually, Lisa was the one who wanted to surprise you this morning."

His face brightened again. "Okay. Give me ten minutes to shower and shave."

"We'll wait in the car."

As they turned to leave, he said, "How about I call that deli up the road and see if they can pack us a picnic basket. Sub sandwiches, chips, drinks?"

"No, thanks," Lisa said. "We packed bottled water and granola bars."

"But we'll probably be gone through lunch."

"And we might get so into the hiking that it'll be hours before we're ready to stop," Lisa said. "Your turkey on rye will be crawling with salmonella by then."

"Well, what about a park pass? Will we need one?"

"We invited you, Uncle Michael. Do you wanna go or not?"

"I'm just trying to help. A little organization never hurt anyone."

"You're, like, about to kill my joy with it. Forget the details. Let's go hike and have fun."

Josie looked back and forth between the two, waiting for the next volley, hoping they could settle it themselves. Instead, they

125

stood, silently fuming, hands jammed on hips, a mirror image of each other.

Josie sighed. "Let's go wait in the car, Lisa. Mike, be sure to wear comfortable walking shoes."

"I may need to stop and buy some hiking boots. These are my running shoes, but . . ."

Lord, give me patience. And help them both quit being so hardheaded.

Josie shepherded Lisa out the door and closed it on Mike's plea for boots. Someone had to get them moving along or it would be dinnertime before they got there.

CHAPTER SIX

As Josie took them on the short drive toward the national park, Mike — who'd had his offer to drive refused so had gotten stuck in the backseat — leaned over and pointed. "Hey, there's a place that might sell boots."

"Forget it," Lisa said from the copilot's position in the front passenger seat.

"There goes my chance at decent footwear."

He said it so wistfully, Josie almost laughed.

"The mud will ruin my new running shoes."

Josie had seen them earlier. Brand-new, top of the line, with chambers of air cushioning each step. "How often do you run?"

"Every Monday, Wednesday, Friday. Three-point-two miles."

Lisa snickered and looked at Josie as if

to say see?

"Three-point-two, huh? Never three? Or three and a half?" Josie asked.

She glanced at him in the rearview mirror. His slow-forming, knowing smile sent a buzz clear down to the toes of her hiking boots.

"No, ma'am. Never. Three-point-two, exactly three times a week. Every week." He rubbed his chin. "Except today."

Instead, today you were standing in the motel doorway, your rugged, casual look sending my pulse on a three-point-two-mile run.

In about one minute.

Josie steered into the Great Smoky Mountains National Park and drove upward, looking for a more secluded scenic overlook. One without so many cars.

"Let's stop somewhere near the river," Lisa said. "I want to climb on the rocks."

They drove through the emerald-green scenery, lush with new growth and newly blooming wild dogwood trees, and pulled alongside the road to park in a deserted area. When they climbed out, the cool, misty air seemed to envelop them. Trees surrounded them so they could barely see the sky — their own little fairyland.

Josie breathed in the damp, woodsy scent.

"It's so beautiful, I hate to speak and spoil it."

"I don't mind," Lisa said, much louder. "Come on. Let's climb down to the river."

"What about the drinks?" Mike walked around to the trunk. "Do you want me to get the cooler?"

Josie laughed. Did the man think they were going to let him die of thirst? "No. We can get it later. Let's catch up with Lisa before she does something silly like dive in."

Once they'd hiked down the bank to the edge of the water, they found Lisa standing on a large rock. She leaned toward the next one, as if trying to jump rock to rock.

"Lisa, that's dangerous. Come on over here with us," Mike said.

"I'm fine. I have, like, the best balance of anyone I know."

Josie's heart skipped a beat as Lisa leaped and nearly missed. One big black combat boot dipped into the rushing water. "Oops."

Mike lunged, as if to grab her. "Lisa. Come back here this instant. Those boots aren't made for climbing."

"It's not deep, Uncle Michael."

"But you could crack your head on one of those slick, mossy rocks."

"Lisa," Josie said, her own fear growing. "Do what your uncle says."

"I didn't come here just to stand and look at it."

"We can wade at the edge of the water," he said.

Lisa laughed as she threw her arms out to balance another near miss. "I dare you to take off your shoes and stick your feet in this ice-cold water."

"I'm not a fool. Now come —"

"Your lily-white toes probably haven't seen the light of day since you were five."

Even though Lisa was talking big, she had started toward the bank. Able to take a deep breath at last, Josie plopped herself down in the grass.

Lisa returned to the big rock at the edge of the water, faced the sky with arms out, then began to twirl around. "I love it here. Cool, fresh air. Not a musty dorm room in sight."

As she spun, Mike inched toward her, his hands out to catch her in case she fell. As soon as she stopped and looked down, he jerked his hands back to his sides.

His actions twisted Josie's heart. He truly did care for his niece and was trying to approach her on her terms. No more sudden hugs. He knew he couldn't just grab Lisa and pull her off the rock.

The look of insecurity on the face of a

man who Josie imagined had never experienced such a thing in his life made *her* want to grab *him* and hug.

She knew how it felt to try so hard, then to have it thrown right back in your face. She'd often hugged her parents only to have them shrug off her affections.

Huge outbursts of emotion weren't *seemly.*

Lisa hopped off the rock — finally — and pulled her boots off. Socks followed, tossed over her shoulder. "Okay, Uncle Michael. Time to air out the toes."

He glanced at Josie. She smiled at him and shrugged. "You got yourself into this one. You can't complain since she's in one piece on dry land again."

"You're exactly right." He sat by Lisa and without any hesitation, pulled his shoes and socks off, then rolled up his khaki pants to just below his knees.

His feet weren't pale at all. They were nearly as dark as his tanned face and arms. She should have known the man wouldn't have imperfect feet.

Lisa was already in the water past her ankles. "Oooh, it's freezing!"

"Okay, here goes." Mike stepped in, and sucked in a quick breath.

"Man, I'm numb already," Lisa said.

Mike tried to step deeper, but said, "Oh, oh, ouch," as he hopped from foot to foot.

Maybe his too-tender feet weren't so perfect after all.

Lisa watched as he continued to hop around. A grin seemed to sneak up on her, then her shoulders started to shake. Finally, she gave in and howled with laughter. The kind of laughter a teenager should indulge in every day. The kind Josie hadn't heard out of Lisa yet.

Something that had been tight within Josie let loose. *This is the way it should be, Lord. Lisa happy. Mike and me having fun. Like a family should be.*

A family? A chill as cold as the river water had Josie up off the ground and heading up the hill. Had she really placed herself in that loving picture? She who had no idea what it really meant to be part of a normal family?

"Where're ya going?" Lisa hollered.

"I, uh. I'll be right back."

A family? Yes, Lisa and Mike. They were a unit. Why should that send fear racing to her heart?

She was acting crazy, just plain weird. Josie opened her car trunk and pulled out the cooler, then grabbed a blanket. After lugging it down the hill, she took off her boots to join them, trying to forget her over-reaction.

She climbed up on Lisa's big rock.

"Whoa." Mike made his way through the water to take her hand. "Here, I don't want to see your head cracked, either. You're not quite as young and agile as Lisa."

"Now, how am I supposed to take that comment, Mike?"

Another one of those dreaded slow smiles pulled at his lips and sparkled in his deep blue eyes. "I guess I would take it as an insult. What about you?"

"You big oaf." She shoved at him with the hand he was gripping, pushing him off balance.

He tried to let go of her, but she held tight, trying to steady him. Unfortunately, he was too heavy for her. His feet went flying out from under him, and he yanked her off the rock as he landed on his rear in the water. She landed beside him on her hands and knees, banging her right knee on a protruding rock.

All she could do was huff, trying to catch the breath that had been frozen out of her. But Lisa's hysterical laughter brought reason back to Josie's frosted brain. She slowly straightened, weighted down by sopping clothes and a throbbing kneecap, and offered Mike a hand.

"I'm afraid I can't move. I've become a chunk of ice," he said.

"That's what you get for calling me old and stiff." She reached and found his hand in the water. With a tug, she helped him up. They ended up about six inches apart, smiling like idiots.

They stood like that for too long, yet she couldn't resist. With slight pressure, he began to pull her toward him. But before her body would follow, he pushed her away and let go. The grin faded, and he glanced at Lisa.

"Hey, you two. Let's get going. I'm cold." Lisa's arms were crossed tightly in front of herself once again. She glared at them as if they had committed a crime.

Close to it. Josie knew he had been about to kiss her. Had Lisa noticed?

As Josie climbed out of the water, Mike held out his hand to help her. She acted as if she hadn't seen it. Lisa marched up the hill, and Mike took the blanket and wrapped it around Josie's shoulders.

He untucked his shirttail from his waistband and squeezed out the water. "Go on up, Josie," he said without looking at her. "I'll bring the cooler."

"Sure. Okay." She had no idea what to say, so she started toward the car. Lisa turned and shot daggers her way.

Once she and Lisa had closed themselves inside Betty's warmth, she in the front and Lisa in the back, Lisa said, "I saw the way you two looked at each other."

"I don't know what you mean."

"Yeah you do."

"We were just goofing off."

"It was more than that this time. You've looked at him like that before. But now he's all interested in you, too."

"Lisa!"

"He'll hang around for you, now."

"Your uncle is here for you. Totally."

"Come on, Josie. What does he truly want with me? He's here because he has to be, and you know it."

"He loves you."

"He's Mr. Responsible. That's the only reason he bothered to find me."

"Look, your uncle and I are as different as night and day. Sure, we may cause a few sparks to fly. But that's it. It's all in fun."

Lisa slouched in the backseat, silent.

"I promise you, Lisa, that's all there is to it. Your uncle is an old stick-in-the-mud, and I couldn't ever fall for him."

Hope shone in Lisa's eyes. "You promise? 'Cause once he and Gloria started seeing each other, I never heard from him."

So he and Gloria had seen a lot of each other, huh? "I promise. We'll all hang out together. But that's it. No relationship between Mike and me."

A sigh escaped Lisa as Mike opened the car door and slid the cooler in beside her.

"Let's get home," he said. "Or we'll all have pneumonia."

Josie started the car and put the heat on high. Her teeth began to chatter. But it wasn't one hundred percent from the dunking.

Lord, help me here. I can't afford to think of Mike as anything other than a business relationship. And our business is Lisa's welfare.

The next morning, Michael sat in the diner drinking coffee that Bud had brought him. Josie seemed to be hiding in the kitchen.

No wonder. He'd been a brute the day before. He'd practically dragged her to him to kiss her, right there in front of Lisa.

Now Josie avoided him like a bad case of food poisoning.

"G'morning, Uncle Michael." Lisa climbed in across from him.

"Good morning."

At least Lisa had greeted him. She'd even given him a tentative smile. And he could

136

live with that.

Forget Josie.

Speaking of Josie . . . She walked out of the kitchen, grabbed a plate from Bud and plunked it down in front of him. "Here's your breakfast."

She stalked away, bracelets clanging in time to the sway of her hips. Once she reached a table across the room — where the same construction workers sat every time he'd been in the diner — she parked herself right beside the bearded giant.

After a few minutes, Josie went back to work and didn't pay Lisa and him an ounce of attention other than to refill his coffee and to bring Lisa a plate of fruit with one hard-boiled egg.

"Go ahead and take your break," Josie told Lisa without acknowledging him. "You can eat with Mike."

"Is that all you're going to eat?" he asked.

"I usually eat fruit, but Josie makes me eat an egg sometimes, too."

"Well, good for Josie. You need some protein."

Lisa worked diligently to crack the eggshell on the edge of her plate, avoiding eye contact. "So, you like her, huh?"

"I beg your pardon?"

A repeat of the tension of yesterday stiff-

137

ened her shoulders. "Josie. I saw the way you looked at her at the park. You like her. As more than a friend."

"I don't have feelings for anyone."

"Yeah, right. And you weren't just looking jealous, either."

Michael still couldn't figure out Lisa's attitude change. All he knew was that the near-kiss had incited it.

"I'm not jealous, either," he said.

"Then why were you scowling at Butch?"

"Butch?"

"The guy Josie sat by."

"He seemed to be flirting with her."

"So? They're buddies. They went out once, but there wasn't any oomph there."

"Oomph?"

"Yeah, that's what Josie called it. It's just like what you two have for each other."

She looked at him expectantly, as if hoping he would deny it. He sipped his coffee, unsure how to handle this newest dilemma. There was definitely unexplainable oomph between him and Josie. But how would that affect Lisa?

"So, what do you think about Josie?" he asked to test the waters.

Lisa mashed a clump of eggshell, then focused on rolling a grape around her plate. "She's my friend. She took me in and helped me get a job."

"What if I was attracted to her?"

Lisa shrugged, but the way she clutched at her elbows — that and the fact that she'd pushed away her uneaten food — told him it was feigned nonchalance.

"I admit there's some chemistry between us," he said. "But that's all. She's got her life here, and we have ours in Charleston."

Lisa's posture eased. She picked up a grape and popped it into her mouth. "Yeah, I guess we do have our life back home." She sat up a little straighter. "I mean, *you* do. Me — I mean, I don't know what I'm going to do. But you're here now . . . for me. Right?"

He nodded. Unable to speak, he cleared the lump out of his throat. "Yeah, I am."

Once he and Lisa had finished breakfast, Michael paid the bill and tipped Josie better than usual since she was taking care to make sure Lisa had nourishing food.

"I guess I should get back to washing dishes," Lisa said.

"Thanks for eating with me. I hate to eat alone."

"You do?"

"Yes. Unfortunately, I eat most of my meals at my desk or on the road."

"You never told me that."

"It never came up, I guess."

"If I'd known, maybe I wouldn't have told you no when you invited me to dinner that time. Maybe next time I can, like . . . well, when I come visit Charleston, I can go eat with you. If you want."

Come for a visit? Did he dare hope this was a step in the right direction? He'd better tread carefully. "Thank you. That's really sweet of you to offer."

That sounded awful, Michael. Can't you do better?

The crease in Lisa's brow confirmed his stupidity.

"I'll be sure to take you up on that sometime," he amended.

She looked at him, searching for the truth.

"Soon," he added quickly. "Once you come home."

"How soon?"

Ouch. She certainly had him pegged — busy schedule and all. And it showed just how negligent he'd been. He took out his electronic organizer. "Let's see. . . ."

"What're you two planning?" Josie asked from out of nowhere. He hadn't even heard her squeaky shoes or jewelry.

Lisa looked at the ceiling and sighed in the irritating, sarcastic way that was becoming far too familiar. "Supposedly, a meal together in Charleston. Someday," she answered.

Here it comes. The dressing-down from Josie.

Instead, Josie gave him a wide-eyed, shocked look. Then she smiled. "How nice!" Josie scooted Lisa over and sat plastered against her. "How about at Magnolia's?"

He squinted at her over the organizer. "You've been there?"

"Yes, just once. A really long time ago."

"You never mentioned you've been to Charleston."

"Oh, I've been all over the place. Pretty much a drifter until I settled here two years ago."

"Josie, you'll have to come and meet us there sometime when I'm visiting Uncle Michael." Animation subtracted years off Lisa's face.

"We'll see, sweetie. You know how much Bud needs me here. Especially since he hurt his back."

Michael placed the stylus back in its slot. "He was injured?"

"Fell off a ladder," Josie said. "Now he's decided to retire."

"Josie's saving to buy the diner from him," Lisa said.

"Lisa, let's not get into that right now."

"Have you tried to get a loan?" he asked.

She laughed and swatted her hand in the air. "I'm not going to discuss my financial situation with you two."

Lisa leaned toward her uncle. "That's why she's so thrifty. She saves every penny. Literally."

"I see."

"Seriously," Lisa continued despite Josie's elbow in the ribs. "She has a piggy bank in the kitchen at home."

Michael sat back and stretched his arms along the vinyl booth. "That'll take a while, I guess."

Josie huffed. "Don't be ridiculous. It's not all my savings. It's just my thankful box."

"Every time she's thankful for something, she puts some change in it," Lisa said.

"That's a great thing to do." He'd always admired people with positive attitudes, and had vowed on more than one New Year's Eve to be more of an optimist.

A blush lit Josie's face. She'd never looked prettier. "It's just something I read about. So I figured why not do it to add to my savings account."

"That's why she didn't want to use her thankful money, even when she ruined her hair."

"I see. The plot thickens."

"Okay, Lisa. Time to start being a normal, closemouthed teenager." Josie laughed, seeming uncomfortable with Lisa's honesty.

Michael found it very intriguing. "No, go on, Lisa. I want to hear the story about the hair."

Josie patted her fluffed-up hairdo. It looked like a ponytail that had exploded into a fountain of pink. "I'm going back to work. You two need to find something better to talk about."

She hurried away, that fountain of hair bobbing up and down.

Lisa leaned closer, as if to confide in him. She hadn't wasted a second warming to the new topic. Apparently, she didn't feel so threatened by Josie anymore. Or else she was going to reveal something that might harm his opinion of Josie.

"When I first found the diner," she said, "the guy I'd come with had just dumped me. For some, skinny black-haired model-type. I was furious."

"I imagine so. Plus he *had* stolen your car."

"Oh, that didn't bother me as much as the fact that he'd asked me to marry him, then took up with that tramp as soon as he found out I wouldn't sleep with him."

Michael's face burned as he studied paint

peeling off the wall in the corner.

"Oh, don't be such a dork, Uncle Michael. It happens all the time."

"Not to you, I hope."

"No. I know better. I'm holding out till marriage."

He swallowed. Parenting — well, being a guardian, rather — wasn't for cowards. Or for dorks, like him. "Smart decision. I'm glad."

"Anyway . . . I'd just been dumped for the black-haired tramp. So the first night at Josie's, I was bawling my eyes out. So she suggests we color our hair."

"Did she suggest green, then?" He'd have a word or two for her if she had.

"No, it was already green, which, by the way, hadn't gone over too well at school. But the roots had grown out. Once we got to the drugstore, I talked her into trying red. I don't think she would have ever done it if it weren't for me crying right there in the hair-color aisle. I mean, it was a bad scene."

Michael's mind raced to keep up with his suddenly talkative niece. "So how did her hair end up pink? And what does this have to do with the piggy bank?"

"Chill out. I'll get to that part." She leaned her arms on the table, eyes alight with mischief. "She didn't have any other cash with her. And the green was expensive. So there we were counting her quarters and dimes and pennies. We were cutting it close. And since I couldn't risk using my credit card, I wasn't any help at all."

He tried to look stern. "No, you couldn't risk your uncle finding you."

"Never." She smiled a pleased smile. "So we put back her ten-dollar box of burnt-auburn and got a generic brand out of the clearance bin. The only red they had on sale for three dollars was strawberry-blond."

"Oh, no."

"Since Josie's real hair is, like, medium brown, well, you can guess what that blond kit did."

"Bleached it?"

"Bleached it and turned it the color of a strawberry."

Michael tried to imagine what a woman would do in that situation. The picture wasn't pretty. "I hope she didn't fuss at you."

"Fuss? Not at all. For a minute or two, I thought she might cry. She stood silent, staring at her hair. Her eyes even watered. But then all of a sudden, she smiled. 'I used to have a strawberry-scented doll that had hair this color,' she said. 'I loved that doll more than any other because it was the only doll my dad ever picked out for me.' "

The story served as a punch to his gut. Could Lisa possibly know how much she'd just told him about Josie? "She said that, huh?"

"Yep. Then she went and washed it about fifty times to get some of the pink out. The next morning, it looked pretty much like it does now."

"And she wouldn't go to a salon to get it repaired because she's cheap."

"Cheap?"

"That's what she told me."

"Oh, she's never cheap. She's spent money on me. But she won't spend it on herself. Anyway, she says she likes being different for a change."

Different. Yes, she was much different from what he had thought. From how he had judged her to be.

If it weren't for the kindness she'd shown Lisa, Josie would still have nice brown hair to match her beautiful brown eyes.

And what had *he* offered his niece? Lisa's own flesh and blood had repeatedly sent her off to school to let someone else deal with her while a total stranger had sacrificed her own self-image to make the girl feel important.

He looked at the girl across from him, who looked exactly like the sister he missed so much, and he knew, for the first time in years, what it felt like to be lucky. A bond had begun to form between him and Lisa.

But he feared a bond had begun to form between him and Josie, also. Yet he couldn't act on it. Lisa had to be his number-one priority. Lisa, who, for some reason, didn't want him to have any feelings for pink-haired Josie Miller.

CHAPTER SEVEN

Okay, back to business. No more letting herself get caught up in discussions about her goals, her dreams. Or her piggy bank.

Josie was going to stick to a plan to teach Mike how to take care of his niece. He would have Lesson Number One: A lesson in shopping. The ultimate teenage pastime. And he would learn at the mall.

Once the three of them arrived at the mall in a neighboring town, Mike stood at the entrance as if scared to go in.

Josie gave him a shove. "You're safe. No one bites."

Lisa observed the two of them, so Josie made sure there wasn't a trace of attraction on her face — no staring, no pudding knees, no drooling. She would keep herself at least a foot away from him from now on.

"All right, here's our plan." She pulled a wadded napkin from the pocket of her denim skirt. She'd scribbled a list earlier.

"First, Lisa needs some new jeans."

"My jeans are fine," Lisa said.

"We could send for her things from the school," Mike suggested.

"She needs something for work besides those baggy pants that drag on the ground. The bottoms of the legs stay wet."

Mike rubbed his hands together. "I agree with you there, Josie. Where to?"

"This is starting to look like you two ganging up on me," Lisa said. "Remember what I said about that?"

Josie tucked the list back into her pocket. "This isn't ganging up. We just agree on something for a change."

"Yes, take note, Lisa. This may be a first."

"And a last, I hope," Lisa snapped.

As much as Lisa objected, she didn't seem to mind once they got to the store. Fortunately, Josie had called ahead to make sure this store sold something besides those ill-fitting jeans.

Lisa hunted through several racks, then finally pulled out a hanger.

"Those look like they'll drag on the ground, too," Mike said.

"Maybe not. Just let me try them on."

"Go ahead, Lisa," Josie said.

Lisa gave him an exaggerated, smart-alecky smile and hurried off.

149

"Why did you allow her to try on that huge pair?"

"Believe it or not, they look smaller than her usual jeans."

"I can tell by looking at them on the hanger that they're too long."

"Well, she needs to learn to shop for what's appropriate. And you need to learn how to say no and redirect her — in a nice way that'll be easy for her to swallow." She gave him her sweetest smile, knowing how difficult that task would be.

He practically snorted at her comment. "Yeah, we'll see."

After ten minutes, Mike paced the floor. "Shouldn't you go check and make sure she hasn't been kidnapped?"

Josie cackled. "Good one, Mike. You're too cute."

"Cute? I'm serious."

"Oh, well . . ." She checked her laughter. "You'll learn. These things take time."

"How long could it possibly take to try on one —"

Lisa stepped out of the fitting room. "Well?"

"They fit nicely." Josie signaled for Lisa to spin around. "Mike, what do you think?"

Josie could imagine he wanted to say "Too long," and be done with it.

"Will they work for the diner?" he said, instead.

"I don't know," Lisa said. "They drag on the ground a little."

Mike pointed. "And they do look —" he gestured at the distressed areas of the denim "— used."

"They're supposed to, Uncle Michael."

"How do they feel?" Josie asked.

"Great."

"Do you think you could find a trimmer style that might be more appropriate for work?" he asked.

Way to go, Mike. Leading instead of ordering her.

"I guess I can try some. But I won't promise anything." She went right to her size on the shelves along a wall, pulled out a folded pair of what appeared to be a more traditional style, then headed back into the dressing room.

"I'm proud of you, Mike. I wasn't sure you had it in you."

"Despite what you might think, I am teachable."

"And you're a quick learner, too."

After several minutes, Lisa reappeared. "These may be okay." She examined herself from all angles. "You don't think they make me look fat, do you?"

"You don't have an extra ounce of fat on your body," Mike said.

"Your weight is just right for your height, Lisa. Those look great."

"They're perfect for the diner. They look good on you," he said.

"They're really different, but I think I can get used to them." She seemed pleased at how she looked.

She really did have a nice figure buried under all those baggy clothes, belts and chains. Josie hoped she might realize it and gain some self-confidence.

"Can I buy them, Uncle Michael?" she asked.

"Of course we can buy them. Go get two more pairs and we'll meet at the front of the store."

After Lisa changed and picked up the extra jeans, she met them at the checkout line.

Josie nodded toward the store exit. "Come on, Lisa. While Mike pays, let's go look for a belt at that little accessory shop."

He pulled out his wallet. "I imagine a plain leather belt would look nice."

"I've got to have *some* way to express myself," Lisa said as if the traditional jeans were almost too much to bear.

He smiled at her. "Go, then. I wouldn't

want to crush your identity."

He'd said it so sweetly that Josie wanted to hug him.

Maybe he could succeed at this shopping after all.

Michael was relieved to have the shopping ordeal over. But it hadn't been as painful as he'd feared it would be.

Not once had he upset Lisa. And Josie seemed proud of his effort. Of course, she'd been along to help. He hoped to be as successful when it was just him and Lisa.

As he walked the area near the denim store waiting for Lisa and Josie to return, he meandered into a jewelry boutique. The items appeared to be designed by the owner and handmade. He immediately thought of Josie.

"May I help you?" the sales clerk asked.

"I'm just browsing."

"Let me know if I can answer any questions."

Once he'd made a trip around the small shop, he knew that Josie could make several items with quality just as good. "Excuse me," he said.

"Yes?"

"Does the owner make your entire inventory, or do you purchase from other suppliers?"

"Most of the pieces are made by the owner. But we do take some on consignment. Mostly from students at the craft school in Gatlinburg."

From the prices he'd seen, Josie would be able to buy the diner a lot sooner if she could sell some of her work in a retail outlet like this one. "I know someone who makes wonderful pieces. Could I give her one of your business cards?"

She handed him a card. "Of course. We'd love to see them."

"Thank you." On a whim, he pointed at the nearest display case. "I'd like to see that amber necklace-and-earring set. . . ."

Michael sat on a bench surrounded by lost-looking men. Some snoozed. Some read the newspaper. Others looked as bewildered as he felt.

How long could it take to buy a belt?

He heard Josie's laughter before he saw her. Then Lisa's followed. The two had probably been up to no good.

"Hey, Uncle Michael. Wanna see my new belt?" She lifted it out of a shopping bag. It was leather — with large metal studs all around, like a collar you'd expect to see on a vicious junkyard dog.

154

He stood and checked out the men around him. None seemed fazed. They probably all had mall-dwelling daughters. "That's nice. Not a single chain link."

Lisa laughed. "What about Josie's? I talked her into getting a belt, too."

Josie swatted at Lisa. "You did not."

"You're right. I didn't talk you into it, you did it all on your own." A devious laugh bubbled out of her. "Go ahead. Show him."

Josie took hers out of a shopping bag. "I couldn't resist. I thought it was cute." The belt was all metal, made of small, delicate chain links, just like Lisa's old belt — only a smaller version.

Michael had to laugh. It looked as if Josie wanted to express herself as well. Just more daintily.

"It'll give her something to remember me by," Lisa said.

Encouraged that she might be thinking in terms of going home eventually, he said, "Yes. A souvenir from your visit."

"I'm wiped out," Lisa said. "Let's get out of here."

"Fine with me," Josie said.

"Oh, before we go." He gave Lisa her bag with the jeans, then took the small bag and handed it to Josie. "This is to thank you for bringing me along to learn about shopping for Lisa."

"Oh. Wow. I don't expect anything." Her expression faded.

"I know. But you've done so much for us. I wanted to do something in return."

She pulled the box out and opened it. He didn't know what he'd expected, but it wasn't the tightness that pulled across her cheekbones, or the drawn circle of her mouth. "I can't accept this."

It was as if a sudden artic wind had blown through the shopping mall, chilling everyone in their little circle of three. He looked to Lisa to explain, but she gazed off at who knew what.

"But I picked them just for you. They're handmade. The stone is amber."

"I know that. You also got them right there." She pointed. "At that expensive boutique."

"I thought —"

"Once again, you're trying to pay me for something I've wanted to do."

Michael wished a hole would open up and swallow him. What had he been thinking, buying her a gift she could make by herself, as if he could ever fully pay her back? "I'm sorry. I should have thought."

"No problem. Just don't try to pay me again, okay?"

"Sure. Okay."

"I'm going to the car. Can I have your keys?" Josie asked. "You two can catch up with me."

He held them out to her. She took them, shoved the bag back into his hands, then stalked away.

"I thought you said you didn't want a relationship with Josie," Lisa said.

"I don't."

"Duh. Get a clue. A guy buys jewelry when he loves the girl."

He'd hurt Lisa. He could tell by the slump of her shoulders. And he had offended Josie as well. How could one little gift cause such upheaval?

Apparently, he was clueless. Or just insensitive.

"It was merely a nice gesture," he said. "Nothing more." His motives had been pure. Hadn't they?

"Yeah, right." She thumped the side of his head. "You need to use that big brain of yours, Uncle Michael." She smiled as if to try to take the sting out of her words. "Use it to think. You know, that basic human trait?"

The resemblance was uncanny. Lisa, telling him he was not human. His sister, telling him he was unfeeling, incapable of loving — right before she drove off in a drunken rage and careened into a telephone pole.

Josie slouched in Mike's smooth, leather interior, fighting tears. Lisa walked out of the mall and was searching for the car, so Josie had to get a grip.

She swiped at her eyes. It was funny how she could go ages without crying. She was steel, even through Hallmark commercials. But anger . . . that was what really turned on the faucets.

I refuse to be bought. Never again.

That was what her refusal boiled down to. Everything always came back to her parents. Especially her dad.

Irritated at Mike, Josie twirled her bracelets and tapped her foot. How had he known the exact pieces she had wished for?

He couldn't have known. Which irritated her even more. Without a clue, he'd bought the very necklace and earrings she'd coveted for months. They were going to be her reward for saving enough for a down payment on the diner. They were going to be a celebration gift to herself.

Now he would probably toss them into his car and forget about them. Or he'd give them to someone else.

She wanted to howl in disappointment, in frustration, as Lisa opened the door and sat beside her.

"There you are. I couldn't find you," Lisa said.

"I needed some peace and quiet. Where's Mike?"

"Getting a Coke. Are you mad at him because jewelry is such a girlfriend-boyfriend thing?"

"I just don't appreciate gifts given for the wrong reasons. It brings back hurtful memories — of being bought off by my dad."

"If Uncle Michael was buying you off, he'd pull out a wad of money, not go get you something at a jewelry store."

"You wouldn't understand, Lisa."

"Wanna bet? I always get the Christmas, birthday and Easter guilt-offerings. And he never once got *me* something handmade, something that he picked out."

Josie's conscience pricked. Plus, her faucets were trying to turn on again.

"Enough," Josie said. "Hop out and watch for Mike. He'll probably get lost trying to find us."

Michael couldn't believe Josie had invited him into her home after the way she had acted at the mall. Yet here he sat at one end of the couch with her at the other. He also couldn't believe he had been stupid enough to buy her such a personal gift. As Lisa had said, jewelry usually meant something serious, not merely thank you.

But one minute he had been in the shop looking at the amber set, comparing it to Josie's pieces of jewelry, then the next he'd been picturing her wearing it.

The stones were set in dangly silver, and he always thought of amber as a slice of history. It had seemed like a combination Josie would like.

Stupid, stupid, stupid.

"Thanks for letting me come inside to tell Lisa goodnight," he said.

"No problem." She seemed ready to say something more but stopped.

"I should probably get back to my room and check in with Gary."

"Gary?"

"My brother. He's filling in for me at the bank. I need to check in on a new construction loan."

"Business must be good."

"It is. And Gary just reeled in a reluctant new client while I was here."

She studied him until he had to look away.

"I'm afraid I was the problem all along," Michael said. "Gary and Tom must have hit it off at their dinner meeting."

"I'm sorry."

"No, don't be. It's good news. I had been working on him for months."

"Then that must make it even harder."

Why was she trying to take something positive and make it sound as if it had hurt his feelings? It hadn't.

A tightness in his chest reminded him otherwise. "I guess you're right. It's hard on the pride."

He observed the funky picture on the wall once again. Then he slapped his legs. "Well, I should go. You've got an early morning tomorrow, I'm sure."

As he rose from the couch, she put her hand on his arm and guided him back down. "Stay for a minute. I need to talk to you about the necklace and earrings."

"I'm really sorry about offending you with the gift," he said, wondering why she'd brought it up again.

Her big brown eyes appeared very serious. "No. I shouldn't have overreacted. It's just that my dad always bought me gifts."

Michael didn't get the connection.

"But they were only to make up for him never being around. They were a pitiful substitute for the affection I needed so badly."

"Were your parents divorced?"

She chuckled, but it was more a sound of irony. "No. But it's a miracle they weren't. He worked all the time. And traveled lots."

"That's interesting," Michael said. "My dad did the same thing. Either that, or he took me to the bank with him to assuage his parental guilt."

He remembered being six years old, waiting for his father to come out of a long meeting in the boardroom. "I hated it."

"I'm sorry," she said for about the third time. "I reacted to my old insecurities when, really, my main concern is that I don't want Lisa feeling as if you've bought my friendship for her."

"I can understand that. Thanks for explaining. I'm just sorry for bringing up bad memories for you this evening."

"I'm okay. Don't worry about it."

"I have no idea why I bought you the jewelry in the first place. I never buy gifts. I always send my secretary to do it."

She smiled, lifting the heaviness from the room. "I'm impressed. You showed more spontaneity than I've given you credit for."

He laughed. "You're right. And I enjoyed it. Oh, I almost forgot." He reached into his wallet and pulled out the business card. "I talked to the woman working at the boutique today about how talented you are. She said she would be willing to look at your work. They sell some on consignment."

Josie sucked in her breath.

"Now, before you get mad at me for interfering in your business, let me say that you could make the money to buy the diner a lot sooner if you sold jewelry on the side."

"Did she really say I could contact them?"

"She really did. And you should have seen the prices on bracelets similar to yours."

"I know." Josie grinned. "I have a confession to make."

With that smile, he couldn't imagine it was anything too horrible. "Okay. Fess up."

"I've been in that jewelry boutique many times. In fact, I've admired several pieces by that artist."

"Then you know how high the markup is."

She hesitated. "There's more."

One side of his mouth quirked up. "Then by all means, do tell."

Her gaze darted to the front door. "I've wanted that amber necklace and earrings for months."

"You're kidding."

"No, I'm not. Looks like you've got good taste."

Amazing. The silence drew out as she

smiled at him.

"Thank you for talking to the woman," she said almost in a whisper.

He could swear her eyes got teary. But she didn't well up and actually cry. "For what? All I did was get a business card for you."

"For saying I'm talented. And for going to the trouble."

His face warmed, and he studied the decor around him. "I would gladly give the necklace and earrings to you now, but I don't want to risk upsetting you again."

"After I treated you so badly, I don't deserve them."

"Nonsense. You deserve the gift for . . . well, just for being Josie Miller."

She laughed like the peal of a bell. "Are you serious? You'd still give them to me after I've been such an ingrate?"

"What would I do with them? They screamed your name as soon as I saw them."

She sobered as she cocked her head to the side. "I know. I thought the same thing the first time I laid eyes on the set."

"Then you have to have them." He hopped up, patted his pocket to find his keys. "Be right back. Don't move."

He hurried outside, retrieved the bag, then bounded back up the front steps. Slightly out of breath, he handed it to her. "You're meant to be together."

She carefully, almost worshipfully, pulled out the velvet box. Once she'd removed the earrings and put them in her ears, she grinned, then shook her head to send them swinging. She removed the necklace and held it up to him. "Would you do the honors?"

He swallowed an irrational lump of fear. He could handle being close to her. "Of course."

She stood and turned her back to him.

He draped the necklace in front of her. "Lift your hair."

Once she did, he struggled to fasten the little hook.

"Can you get it?"

"My fingers are rather large and clumsy for this tiny latch."

Just as she let go of her hair and started to face him, he caught the loop, fastening the necklace in place. "Got it."

She completed turning toward him, still within the circle of his arms. "Thanks."

His hands didn't seem to want to move from under the soft curls at her neck. "You're welcome." He stood there stupidly, having no idea what to do next. She was close enough to —

"Are you thinking of kissing me?" she

asked, head cocked, as if she might ask the time of day.

He snapped his hands back to his sides. Had he been that easy to read? She didn't look happy at the prospect, and he couldn't afford to offend her again today. If he did, she might tell him to forget the deal to help with Lisa. "I, uh, I'm sorry. I didn't mean to send that message."

Her eyes narrowed, putting a crease between her troubled brown eyes. He wasn't about to stick around and let his rude behavior mess up what had turned into a nice evening.

"I should go call Gary. Thanks again for taking me shopping with Lisa."

He hurried out the door.

Josie watched the door shut behind him. As she stood there in her dream necklace and earrings, tears scalded her cheeks.

She'd been so sure he was going to kiss her. And, beyond all reason, she'd been thrilled. But then she'd had to open her big mouth, and suddenly he'd been apologizing for sending the wrong message.

Well, which message was true?

It shouldn't matter. I promised Lisa I wouldn't fall for Mike.

She touched the round stone hanging near her heart. *Lord, I'm fed up with this roller coaster of feelings for Mike. One minute, I think he's the worst thing since my dad. Then the next, I think he's the best, most sensitive man, and that maybe You've brought him into my life for a reason. Give me clear vision here. And remind me that my calling is to help Lisa.*

"No more wishy-washy, Josie," she said quietly to the still room. "You've got to stay strong and do everything for Lisa. And Lisa only."

CHAPTER EIGHT

Everything's for Lisa. Everything's for Lisa.
The mantra repeated over and over in
Josie's mind as she searched her closet the
next afternoon after work.

"What's up?" Lisa leaned on the door
frame to Josie's bedroom.

"I'm looking for something for us to wear
tonight."

"For me, too?"

"Yep." Josie tossed a sweater on the bed.

"Why?"

"We're going out to dinner with Mike."

"No big deal. Why change clothes?"

"Because it's time you learn to live in your
world instead of fighting it. Here." She
handed Lisa a plaid wool skirt — timeless,
classic cut, subdued colors.

"Ick."

"Don't 'ick' my old clothes. I was thinner
a few years ago, so they should fit you pretty
well."

Lisa looked at the label. "It's my size." Then her eyebrows arched. "And I recognize the brand."

"I've hung on to a few nice things. From way back."

"Before you started saving for the diner?"

"Yes. Before I even moved here, my mom used to buy only the best. To impress her friends."

"Sounds like Grandmother." Lisa wadded the skirt in her fist. "I guess I could, like, put a cool belt with this thing. And a decent top."

"As long as it's not black." Josie tossed Lisa a pair of tights. "Let's surprise Mike tonight. I've got reservations at a fancy restaurant, so let's try to fit in for a change."

Lisa grinned. "I'll try."

"Lisa. I'm serious about making this night work. Don't do anything to aggravate him."

"Hey, if you'll make yourself fit in, then I'll give it my best shot, too."

As much as it galled Josie to sit in a ritzy restaurant and play the part, she could do it. She might be out of practice, but it would come back to her.

She rooted around near the back of her closet and came up with a gauzy print skirt that hit at her ankles. It would do if she could dress it up. She held it in front of her.

"Whadaya think?"

"It's perfect, Josie. Not too wild, not too stuffy."

Wild and stuffy. Opposite ends of the spectrum. Just like her and Mike.

If she were lucky, Mike would really botch the evening. That way she wouldn't feel drawn to his gentle, more vulnerable side. To his thoughtful side — the one that had brought her the business card.

Of course, thanks to him, she now entertained grand visions of making extra income off something she'd always thought of as a hobby.

Her jewelry.

And that could get her the diner sooner. All her life, she'd wanted to have her very own business. The idea of ordering her world, of being in charge of everything from inventory to payroll, appealed to her.

The diner had fallen into her life at the perfect time. She'd finally been ready to settle in one place. She and Bud had hit it off from day one. He'd even been near retirement and wanted to sell to her.

The restaurant was small enough for her to handle on her own. And she loved the place. Then when the day was done, she looked forward to her beads, her tools, her metals.

She knew, realistically, she couldn't live off the proceeds from selling jewelry. But she could earn a nice income on the side.

All thanks to Mike, who'd had faith in her talent.

Josie jammed the hanger back into the closet. *Botch this dinner, Mike. Please, botch it.*

As Michael knotted his tie, he called to quickly check in with Gary. Mason was still happy, and Michael was able to report a little progress with Lisa. But he had to run. Josie had phoned to say Lesson Number Two was that night — dinner for three. And that he should dress in his church clothes.

He chuckled, picturing them back at the hamburger joint in their Sunday best. His stomach growled as he jogged out to the car. He was supposed to meet the ladies at the restaurant, so he needed to hurry. Josie had said to be prompt. Actually, she'd said, "Don't be late, or I'll make you pick up the tab." Which he intended to do anyway. She'd said she'd made reservations at a nice restaurant. Of course, her idea of nice and his idea of nice might be two totally different things.

After a short drive following Josie's directions, he pulled in the parking lot of the eating establishment. He couldn't tell what kind of place it was from the outside. It was rustic. Quaint. But the quality of food and service would be the deciding factor.

He walked in and peered around. As he approached the hostess station, the door of the restaurant opened behind him. He turned to see a woman walk in. When she looked up, his heart skittered.

It was Josie. At least he thought it was. As she approached — a smile assuring him it was really her — he goggled at her appearance. Her hair was pinned up in some exotic style that left ringlets cascading around her face and neck. Her skirt more than covered her knees and flowed gracefully around her. The blouse had feminine ruffles and a demure neckline. Yet the outfit worked on Josie because it was gypsy-like.

And she wore the necklace and earrings he'd given her.

"Wow." It was all he could manage.

She twirled around. "Thank you."

"Where's Lisa?"

"She's not far behind me. I made her dress up, too."

"Did it infuriate her?"

"More like embarrassed. I reminded her she wouldn't know a soul here."

The door opened, and a panicked Lisa

peeked her green head in. No matter what she wore, it wouldn't change the fact that she had that wild head of hair. Although, she had smoothed it tonight. No spikes.

He motioned her in. She obeyed. And as with Josie, he couldn't believe what he was seeing.

Self-consciously, arms crossed in front of her, Lisa walked to where they stood. She wore the outfit of a prep-school coed. A knee-length plaid skirt. Tailored red blouse. Stockings and flat shoes. The only concession Josie had allowed was a belt that looked like a chain, and not nearly as dainty as Josie's new one. He expected to see a padlock holding it together.

"Wow, Lisa," he said.

"Don't say a word. I know I look stupid."

"Not at all. You look . . ."

"See, you can't even come up with words bad enough."

"No, seriously . . ." He looked past her green hair to the girl. To the young woman who was stripped of her rebellious, protective shell at the moment. A pain knifed his chest. "You look beautiful."

The hopeful look she gave him intensified the stab. "You're not just saying that?"

"No. It's like I can see more of the real you. And you're beautiful."

"So black's not my color?" She smiled and her arms relaxed until she loosely clutched her hands in front of herself.

"I'm afraid not. Though I know you love it."

She shrugged. "I can live without it."

Josie beamed at him. "Then maybe Mike can take you shopping all by himself and get you some nice bright clothes. Red is great on you."

"I'll think about it," Lisa said, fighting a smile.

"We're ready for the Miller party," the hostess said. "Follow me."

The next hour and a half was one of the most pleasant Michael had ever spent. The food was excellent, the service impeccable. And the conversation easy. In fact, it had been rather entertaining.

Josie had been her usual fun self, yet she'd handled the evening as if she weren't at all nervous. He had expected her to be uncomfortable in this setting. Something she'd said previously about going to Magnolia's, though, had made him wonder if she'd dated a man who'd taken her there. Maybe she was used to fine dining from that relationship. The thought gave him pause. Surely they wouldn't have shared such a strong attraction if there was another man in the picture.

"You know, Josie, I've never asked you if you have a relationship that Lisa and I are keeping you from."

Lisa glared at him the way she had that day when he'd gotten too close to Josie in the water. "Uncle Michael, that's none of our business."

Josie waved off Lisa's comment. "It's okay, Lisa. I don't have any special relationships. Just a few good friends."

Was she being vague on purpose? "Friends, huh? Men friends?"

"Quit sounding so pathetic," Lisa said. "We've had such a good time. I mean, it's like we all got along really well tonight. Don't mess it up, Uncle Michael."

"Come on, you two," Josie said. "It's okay. There is no man in my life now. Let's remember that we're here to help Lisa get ready to go home."

Lisa sat straighter, motioned the waiter for more coffee for Michael, then asked for a pot of hot tea. "How am I doing?"

Josie couldn't believe the change. "You're certainly capable of accompanying your uncle to family and business dinners. I guess you have to decide if that's what you want."

Suddenly serious, Lisa looked at Mike. "Did my mom, like, hate all the bank functions and country-club dinners? Is that why she went . . . well, kind of wild?"

He ran his thumb over the rim of his coffee cup. "Honestly, I don't think she ever gave any event half a chance. Seems to me she was unhappy for as long as I can remember."

"Was Grandmother hard on her like she is on me?"

Josie's teeth clenched and she had to force her jaw to relax. *What I wouldn't give to have five minutes with the woman!*

Mike's mouth tilted with an ironic smile. "As impossible as it may seem, your grandmother has learned a lot over the years. She was even harder on your mom. They started fighting around Patricia's twelfth birthday and never stopped."

"Why couldn't Mom just get over it when she was grown up? Why all the booze and stuff — whatever it was that made her look so sick?"

With kind, compassionate eyes, he looked directly into his niece's eyes. "She had lots of emotional problems. Depression. And who knows what else."

"And she used drugs?"

"Yes. But we were never sure what all she was on." He paused. "Can you see why I worry about you now?"

"Do you think Grandmother and Grandfather act like they do because they worry about me like they did my mom?"

He looked thoughtful, as if weighing his words before saying them. "It's different with you. They worry because they love you. They've mellowed a lot since Patricia. With her, they did the best they knew how." He shook his head. "She just seemed born to rebel. She rejected them, their lifestyle, and everything they stood for. They never could seem to get past it and love her anyway."

"Which was what she needed most," Josie said without thinking.

Grief flashed across Mike's face. "You're exactly right."

Then, just as clearly as if God Himself had spoken inside her head, Josie saw that she had done the same thing to her parents. She'd never liked the way they lived their life and had rejected them because of it. She'd run off and never looked back.

Now she knew how that must have hurt them. Even though they had stifled her, had tried to mold her into something she wasn't, she could have reacted better.

Lord, thank You for showing me this. Is this why You brought Lisa and Mike here? To show me that Mom and Dad aren't the only ones at fault in our messed-up relationship?

Josie watched, amazed, as Lisa let Mike touch her arm and didn't move away. It wouldn't be long before he could hug her. Tonight was a big step.

The exquisite dinner sank to the bottom of her stomach like a big blob of oatmeal. The end of their time together was that much closer.

Against their wishes, Michael followed Josie and Lisa back to the house. Once they opened the front door and waved, he drove away, disappointed that they hadn't asked him in. They claimed they were worn out from work, and that they had to get up early. He was probably being paranoid, but he suspected they wanted a girls' night in. Lisa had mentioned something quietly to Josie about a video and popcorn.

Back at his bleak motel room, he tossed his jacket on a chair, removed his tie and unbuttoned the top buttons of his shirt. As he sprawled flat on his back across the bed, he played back his conversation with Lisa. Maybe having more insight into her mother and grandparents would help prepare her for going back home.

Speaking of home . . .

He should probably call his parents to check in.

Instead, he reached for the remote and turned on the television. He hadn't changed the channel from a cable news station since he'd gotten there. He muted it, uninterested in hearing about the bad going on in the world that day.

Dad will expect me to call. But he had kept in touch with Gary. According to him, everything was okay. Michael knew, though, that his dad wouldn't approve.

He kicked off his shoes, then flipped the channels until he found an old movie. Without the sound, the drama was humorous. After a half hour of guessing what the actors were saying to each other, he scrolled up and down the channels once again.

When he landed on an old *Leave It to Beaver* show, he stopped and turned the volume up. After a few good laughs, he hit the off button and got ready for bed.

He climbed under the covers and glanced at the phone. Thinking of going back to twelve-hour days at the bank was depressing. How had he ever thought he could find contentment in that?

It was going to be tough to go back to doing it. But he would. Because it was who he was. It was his duty.

Being gone for the last six days, he'd fallen down on that duty. But now he had a duty to Lisa, as well. And she was much more important, wasn't she? Gary seemed to think so. Surely his parents would agree.

Besides, Gary was thriving. His parents, and the bank, would survive another day without him.

He switched off the light. *It's merely one more day. It's not like I'm leaving the family business.*

CHAPTER NINE

When Michael arrived at Josie's house at 6:00 a.m. the next day, he followed the sound of music and found her on the back deck in the early morning cold, hunched over a book at the table. A cat, maybe the one that had scared him so badly his first night in town, wove in and out, around her legs, trying to brush against them as Josie tried to avoid contact.

He cleared his throat.

No response.

"Excuse me."

"Come back later," she said, intent on her reading.

"What are you doing?" he asked over the music.

"I'm trying to have my devotional time," she said, then huffed a sigh as she leaned back in her chair.

"Oh, sorry. Where's Lisa?"

She turned down the praise music that

sounded vaguely like something he'd heard on a Christian radio station. "Asleep. Go on in."

He entered through the back door into the kitchen. The smell of fresh coffee brewing teased his taste buds.

After passing through into the family room, he approached Lisa's door and knocked.

"Go away," she said in a sleepy voice.

"Time to get up for work."

"You go for me."

"You've got to earn your keep."

"Pay Josie some rent. I'm tired of working so hard."

"Get up. I'll be waiting outside with Josie."

"You won't get her away from her prayer time."

"Then I'll join her."

Lisa's laugh reverberated through the closed door. "I've got to see that."

"Come join us."

He followed his taste buds back to the kitchen and poured two thermal mugs of coffee. He found creamer and sugar on the table and, assuming she used both, doctored her coffee. Once he'd backed out the screen door and placed one cup beside Josie, he sat near her on a cold plastic chair. The cat skittered away at the commotion.

After a couple of minutes, she opened one eye and stole a peek at the cup of coffee. "Amen," she said, then grabbed her mug and inhaled the steam. "Mmm." She took a sip. "It's perfect. Thank you."

"You're welcome."

"Thanks for letting me finish. Why are you here at the crack of dawn?"

"I fell asleep so early last night that I woke up at five this morning."

"Are you getting lonely over at the motel? Because I've got a stray cat I'll gladly loan you for company."

"I'm okay," he said because he hated to admit he'd wanted them to invite him to watch videos last night. "So, do you do this every morning?"

"I try to. When do you pray?" she asked just before sipping her coffee.

"Not often enough. I've found myself praying more lately, though, for guidance with Lisa."

"Good. You two will need lots of prayer when you go back to Charleston together."

"I imagine we will. Will you continue to pray for us, Josie?"

She studied him over her mug, and her eyes looked sad. "Of course. Every day."

Not wanting to think too much about leaving, he stared into the misty backyard.

"It's beautiful out here this time of day."

"Yes. This is my worship time between Sunday services."

"A choir could sure use your talents. Why don't you sing in the one at your church?"

She shook her head, then swallowed another sip. "I've just never taken the step to join, but might do it soon. I definitely feel God's presence in the music. Stayed with me all week."

He smiled, feeling as if he'd accomplished something. "Good. I hope you will."

She stretched her legs out straight and flexed her ankles. "You know, you might enjoy this morning ritual. Try something new, like praise music and prayer on your back deck."

"My housekeeper would faint."

Josie laughed. "So, Mike, has God called you to work at the bank?"

"I have no idea." He'd said it so quickly and definitively that he surprised himself. But he knew without a doubt that he spoke the truth. "I can't say I've ever felt God leading me that way. My family led me into working there. From the time I was about fifteen, I knew that's what I would do. But I suppose God uses our parents to direct us."

"Have you tried asking God what *He* wants for your life?"

"You say that God called you to help runaways. How did you know?"

"Through reading my Bible. Through getting to know God better each day in prayer and by spending time with Him. I don't know. It all just fell into place when my church said they needed someone to help with that ministry."

"So you didn't hear a voice coming from the sky?" He grinned at her, but wouldn't be at all shocked to hear her say she had.

"No. No audible voice. Just confirmation that I was on the right track. Those girls showing up here in town gave me the chance to act."

"So God could have brought me here. Maybe God's calling me to take a bigger part in Lisa's life. But what about my lifetime calling? What about when she's grown and on her own?"

"It might help to focus only on the present. Pray and study the Bible. Get to know God. He'll show you your calling."

Just when Michael thought his course was set, that he had his life in order, God threw in a wrench to remind him He was in charge.

First Lisa had been that wrench. And now Josie was doing the honors.

Unfortunately, Josie was making him think

about a future that might not include the bank. A future with glimpses of more than Throckmorton family duty.

But whatever his calling, Michael felt sure it would lead right back to Charleston. And Josie's call would keep her here in Gatlinburg.

The thought of living 350 miles from this wacky, charming woman left him colder than the early morning fog on this first day of April.

April Fool's, Throckmorton. The joke's on you.

Later, after a busy day at the diner, Josie reflected on how weird sharing the morning with Mike had been. But in a nice way. She'd had an especially smooth day at work. Maybe he'd been praying for her.

And Lisa. Of course he would pray for his niece. His commitment was to Lisa, after all. He didn't owe Josie a thing.

Everything's for Lisa. Everything's for Lisa.

If everything was for Lisa, then why had Josie come home from work and showered with peach bath gel and shampoo, then lotioned up with peach-scented lotion? And why had she put on her best jeans and the aqua-colored sweater that always led to compliments on her brown eyes?

Why had she brushed her teeth twice and left her hair down?

Lisa sure didn't care how Josie smelled or dressed.

Everything's for —

"Let's go, Josie. He'll be waiting."

Surprised to see Lisa standing in the doorway, Josie said, "You're awfully excited to see your uncle."

"I've been doing some thinking about Uncle Michael. I've got an idea about how it'll all work out."

"How?"

Lisa started to put her chain-link belt through the belt loops of her new jeans, but it wouldn't fit. "I've been all wrong about you two."

Josie raised her brows in question.

"Instead of fighting the fact that you two like each other, I'll cash in."

"Cash in, huh? I'm afraid to ask."

"If Uncle Michael falls for you, then you'll be able to talk him into letting me live with him." She shrugged. "I'll just let nature take its course."

This wasn't at all what Josie needed to hear. If she didn't have Lisa fighting the feelings she had for Mike, her heart would be more at risk. "You're kidding, aren't you, Lisa?"

"Nope." Her eyes sparkled. "I've got big plans." She tugged on Josie's arm. "Let's go. You look perfect."

"I don't really care how I look."

"Yeah, right."

"I don't."

"Keep telling yourself that," Lisa said without a hint of the anger she'd had the day they'd fallen in the river and Mike had almost kissed Josie.

Little did Lisa know, Josie had been telling herself that she didn't care how she looked. All afternoon.

It wasn't working.

When they arrived at Mike's motel, he stood outside the office reading a newspaper.

"Sorry we're late, Uncle Michael. Josie was primping."

"Was not."

He leaned toward her and inhaled. "It was worth it. You smell delicious."

Josie studied Lisa's reaction. Where was the disapproval? Was she really over it so quickly?

"Let's go, you two. You can smell each other later," Lisa said.

Mike looked at his niece suspiciously. "Okay. You seem in a hurry."

Lisa grinned. "I just had a really good day,

and I'm looking forward to tonight. Let's go get a funnel cake to share."

"You'll eat some?" he asked.

"Sure. I'm really hungry today."

"What made it such a great day?" he asked.

She took off ahead of them. "Prayer."

Interesting. They walked three blocks to Josie's favorite shop. Lisa stayed about a half block ahead of them the whole way. Josie still couldn't believe the sudden change. While Mike placed their order, she pulled Lisa aside. "What's this about prayer?"

"Whadaya mean?"

"Does all this have to do with what you said earlier? Because I'll try to talk to him about your living with him. I already have. Just don't count on him falling for me."

"It's not only him falling for you." She sank her hands into her pockets, her shoulders slightly hunched. "Last night at dinner was fun. I wouldn't mind us being, well, you know. A kind of family."

Josie's heart nearly jumped out of her chest. She caught herself before she blurted the first thought that came to her mind — one of adamant refusal. "I guess we can act like one for the time you two are here. But remember that it's only for fun. There's no way on earth it could really —"

"Come on, Josie. Give me some credit." Lisa looked away, as if afraid to show Josie the real hope she felt.

This was scarier than anything so far. Lisa could really be hurt when her dream was shattered by reality — like the fact that Josie and Mike lived in two different worlds, and Josie had run from his type of life once.

She and Mike needed to deal with this new problem. And quickly.

When he arrived with the funnel cake, Josie opened her mouth to speak, but Mike's phone rang.

He answered and held it out to Lisa. With a big question mark written across his face, he said, "It's for you."

Lisa smiled with mischief written across her face. "Hello?"

Pause.

"I'd love to. When?"

Pause.

"Now?" she asked, acting surprised but not quite succeeding. "Sure. I'll wait at stop light number six." She handed him his phone.

"Whoever that was sounded scared to death," Mike said.

"It was Brian. He asked me out and is picking me up in a minute."

"What?" Josie said. "You and I are supposed to show Mike the town this evening."

"You two can do it without me. I'm a third wheel."

Josie frowned. Could Lisa, the little matchmaker, be any more obvious?

"Lisa, I'm here to spend time with you," Mike said.

"I know. But you'll get sick of me if you have to spend every day with me. This'll give you a break, and I can go out with Brian. Pleeease?"

"I think she needs to follow through with our plans," Josie said. "Mike?"

"The boy can't seem to keep his hands to himself," Mike warned Lisa.

"Oh, he learned his lesson. I told him we're just friends."

Mike looked at the powdered sugar-coated pastry as if it would tell him what to do, then set the plate on a bench. "If going out with Brian is what you really want to do tonight . . ."

"Yes! Oh, yes." She threw her arms around his neck as she bounded up into his arms. "Thank you!"

He was slow reacting. But not so slow that he missed the chance to hug his niece for the first time in who knew how long. He closed his eyes as he carefully tightened his hold on her. To someone passing by, their embrace would seem to last longer than normal. But to Josie, who knew what a price the two of them had paid for Patricia's carelessness, the long hug, the agonized look on Mike's face, was pure joy.

Josie blinked back tears. When he opened his eyes and gazed at her, she couldn't manage a smile. A smile would only warp and wobble. She bit her bottom lip as it started to quiver.

He sighed as Lisa started to wiggle out of his clutch. Once her feet hit the ground, she pointed down the street. "There's his truck. I'll have him bring me home after the movie."

"Be there by eleven," Mike said.

She picked up the plate holding the funnel cake. "The movie may be at nine."

"Then eleven-thirty."

"Okay. You two have fun." She balanced the plate out in front of her as she darted toward the truck that had pulled to the curb and parked illegally at the intersection.

"Saying thank-you could never be enough. But thank you," he said as he watched Lisa drive off. "You've given me back my niece."

"I didn't do it. God did." *Definitely time for a deposit in my thankful box.*

He looked up to the darkening evening

192

sky. "Thank you, God."

"I'm grateful, too, but we have a new problem. She's acting so perky because she's cooked up a plan to play matchmaker for you and me."

"What?"

"We've got to be careful how we handle this new hope she seems to have about us," Josie said. "She sees it as the solution to you asking her to come live with you."

"We'll deal with it like every other obstacle we've encountered. Right now, I'm too relieved to worry."

He gazed at Josie, fierceness blazing in the midnight-blue. "You've helped me find the Lisa I remember. The Lisa from years ago before my sister started drinking heavily."

"I can't imagine how hard it was for your family."

"The problem is, we didn't deal with it at all. We tried to ignore it, hoping it would go away."

"We all have our skeletons in the closet, Mike."

He sat on a bench and patted beside him. "Tell me your skeletons, Josie."

She joined him, close enough that their legs touched. For some reason, she wanted to talk about her world, her family. "My dad played king of the castle. He ruled over the household with an iron — or as he would claim, godly — hand."

Mike didn't speak, encouraging her to say more. She knew she could trust him with her secrets. He was honorable. Strong. It would be a relief to share what she had never shared with anyone else.

"Like I said the other day, he was gone a lot. When he was in town, he was the model citizen at work and at church — which is what turned me off about going to church when I was young. But at home, he was almost cruel. He was cold. Demanding. My mother scurried around trying to do his bidding."

"Did he physically abuse you?"

"No. Never. But we still feared him. He claimed he treated us that way out of love. Out of a sense of responsibility. But I think he was on some kind of power trip."

Michael had seen his share of power-hungry men. They preyed on those who were weaker. It turned Michael's stomach. "I'm sorry you had to grow up in a situation like that. No wonder you ran away."

"I was just so tired of having to keep my mouth shut. Of having to worry about what I said, who I said it to. You can imagine how hard that was for someone like me who had so much to say." She laughed, but it sounded as if it was out of the pain he imagined she still dealt with.

"I'm glad you got away," he said. "So you could learn to be you."

"That's why I think Lisa needed to get away, mainly from her grandmother. She felt — feels — like she's not able to be herself."

"What about with me?"

"You've done a good job, Mike. Every day she seems more secure with you."

"Thank you, Josie. For everything."

She looked off into the distance and jangled a silver charm bracelet on her left wrist. "I think you're about ready to take her home."

He'd been contemplating the same thing. But every time he would envision driving up to the boarding school, unloading her baggage, hugging her, then saying, "See you next weekend," the picture never balanced with what was in his heart. Nothing about the scene ever added up right.

He couldn't imagine what life would be like with Lisa in it every single day. But he knew he couldn't send her back to school. She deserved a family.

She needs me.

There. He'd thought it, and the earth hadn't stopped spinning.

He stood and crammed his hands in his pockets. Determined to speak the words before he could change his mind, he blurted, "I can't send her back to boarding school."

After taking two seconds to process what he'd just said, Josie grinned and threw her arms around his neck — pretty much the way Lisa had. A split second later, his arms closed around her waist, completing the hug.

"She'll be thrilled," she said.

"Don't get too carried away." He set Josie aside. "I'm not ready to tell her yet, because I'm not sure exactly what to do. I'll take this one step at a time."

She squeezed his arm. "You'll do fine."

"Well, I'd better. It's my fault, you know. The night of the wreck, I told Patricia she was a horrible mother and Lisa would be better off without her."

"Oh, Mike."

"She was crying and probably couldn't see the road."

"You didn't pour the alcohol down her throat. Let it go," she said.

He nodded. "You're right."

He searched up and down both sides of the street, ready to lighten up. It was time to move forward. Time to have some fun.

"What next? You still need to show me the town."

"Pictures. To mark this momentous night."

"Sure. Where to?"

She guided him to a studio that took old-timey photos. They went their separate ways to pick out costumes. Michael couldn't resist dressing as the Wild West version of a banker. As he headed out of the dressing room, he was half-afraid that Josie would show up in one of the skimpy saloon-girl costumes.

But Josie . . . Well, she looked outrageously cute in a bandit outfit with her hair tucked under a cowboy hat, twirling a toy gun around her pointer finger. Chaps fit perfectly with her jeans. She even had on a pair of boots that were about two sizes too big.

Something in his chest twisted around, then settled, as if finding its place for the first time ever. He had to force words past the tightening in his throat. "You look perfect, Josie."

She pointed and laughed at his choice of wardrobe. "I knew it."

The photographer posed them in front of an open safe, then stuffed a bag of coins into Michael's hand.

Josie pointed her gun at him as she fought to look serious. "Stick 'em up."

He raised his bag of "gold," along with his other hand, in surrender.

The camera clicked and flashed. But he didn't bat an eye. As he stared at Josie, he realized he would never need to see the photograph. He knew exactly what it would reveal.

It would reveal the look of utter fear on his face as he surrendered more than gold to Miss Josie Miller.

CHAPTER TEN

After their photo session, Josie said, "Do you mind if we go check on Bud? He's working by himself tonight." She held up the bag of photos. "I'll show him our pictures."

Michael motioned her ahead of him. "I don't mind at all."

After a brisk walk back to his motel, they got in his car and drove to the diner. As they entered, Josie waved at Bud. "How's business tonight?"

"Dead."

"Good. Take a break, and I'll make you a burger." She smiled at Michael. "How 'bout it? Bud's teaching me to make the best burger in town."

"If you say so, then maybe I will."

"You look doubtful. Trust me, Mike. You'll love it."

A smile raised the corners of his mouth. "I seem to be doing a lot of that lately."

"Of what?"

"Trusting you."

She leaned against the counter. "I'll try my best not to fail you."

Considering he'd just admitted to himself that he had feelings for Josie, that was a tall order. "I'm counting on it."

"Here, Bud," she called across to the grill. She waved the bag. "Come see the pics we had made."

Josie handed the bag to Bud, who carefully laid it on the counter so he could wash his hands before handling the photos. Without any hesitation, Josie tossed three hamburger patties on the grill. As Bud examined the pictures, he directed her when to flip and when to press. It was like watching a father teach his child, preparing for passing down the family business — which pretty much seemed to be what was happening.

While Josie intently pressed grease out of the patties, Bud directed his attention to Michael. He stared once again at the old-fashioned photo, then glared at Michael.

Bud leaned over the counter, closer to him. "All I've got to say is don't hurt her. Or you'll have me to tangle with."

"I have no idea what you're talking about."

He gestured toward Josie. "I'm not blind.

And you're not stupid."

Michael did the only thing he could think to do at the moment. He nodded. "Yes, sir."

Bud nodded back. As he eased away, a hand massaging his lower back, he said something that sounded like "She deserves better than you." Then he hollered. "Take 'em off now, Josie. What're ya trying to do, burn 'em up?"

As grouchy as he sounded, Josie grinned at him and came over to pat his cheek. "I'm learning. They get better each time."

Bud gently put the photos back in the bag. As he did so, Michael noticed he took a moment to gaze at the image and almost smile.

Michael knew Bud wasn't admiring *him*. It spoke volumes about the relationship Bud and Josie had, one that Michael hadn't realized until that moment.

So, Josie had found a substitute father, one who was gruff but who truly cared — unlike her own jerk dad. Good for her. *Thank You, Lord, that You provided for Josie.*

Josie gathered the food and shooed Bud away when he tried to carry a plate. "I'll get it. You sit down, and we'll join you."

And thank You for providing for Bud, as well.

"Naw." Bud took the plate from her. "I'll just eat a quick bite in the kitchen if you'll cover out here for me."

"Take your time," she said as the kitchen door flapped closed behind him.

She picked up the spatula and somehow twirled it through her fingers. "I've got more of the town to show you. But first, you need food. Come try the most mouthwatering bite of beef you'll ever taste."

He didn't doubt for a minute that eating a burger lovingly cooked by kind, big-hearted Josie guaranteed the burger would taste better than the finest steak anywhere.

After Michael finished what he said was the best hamburger he'd ever tasted, Josie rested her chin in her hands and studied him as he wiped his mouth on a napkin and took a swig of ice water, draining the glass.

"I had big plans for tonight. Lesson Number Three," she said.

"I'm up for it, now that I've had sustenance."

"It was to teach you to have fun." She smiled at him. "With Lisa."

"Oh. Well, I'm sure you're just as fun as she would be."

"I think the photo session was plenty of fun for the evening. How about we stay here and talk?"

"Sure." He settled back in the booth.

Bud joked with a customer who'd come

in to place a to-go order. Other than that, the diner was empty, no chatter, just the hum of the coolers and ice machine in the distance. "I love it here," she said. "The sounds, the smells, the wild activity during peak times, the lulls like now."

"And one day it'll all be yours."

"Yep. Bud's been letting me take over his duties gradually. The ordering, paperwork, financial aspects."

"Like apprenticing."

"Yes, very much so. By the time I'm ready to get the loan, I should be ready to take over the business."

"So do you think owning this business is God's plan for your life?"

She thought of the many opportunities she'd had in her life, all of which would have earned a good living, would have honored God, but that she had let slip by. "I'm not so sure God's plan was for me to run away and live all the places I've lived. But I do think he's wanted me to bloom where I'm planted, so to speak. I think He approves of what I'm doing with my life now. It may not be His original plan, but I feel like He's using me here, in my church, in my work."

"I guess God uses me in my church work as well, but nothing like what you've been doing by helping runaways."

"I bet you do more than you let on. Lisa mentioned donations to her school. Do you make other donations?"

"Uh, yeah, I give a little here and there — local missions, foreign missions, that type of thing. I help when I can since I've been so blessed." His cheeks reddened. Either in embarrassment or modesty. She would guess the latter.

"My guess is you help a lot."

"Like I said, I've been blessed."

"See, we all play our part."

"But your help is hands-on."

"We all have our gifts. Of course, I'm sure my church could use two more capable hands." She grinned at him, hoping he would think she was teasing. But she was only halfway teasing. She would love for him to stay and to get involved.

With the church. With her ministry to teens.

Who was she kidding? She would love for him to stay and get involved with *her,* too.

"Maybe I'll look for more opportunities to help, hands-on."

Her heart pounded. Could he mean in Gatlinburg? "Great idea, Mike."

Bud clanged around some pots and pans, then started scraping the grill, cleaning it. "I think he's hinting that he wants us to

leave," she whispered. "Time to start clos-
ing."

"Let's offer to help," he whispered back.

"Hands-on ministry?"

He covered her hand with his, and it was
warm. So warm. "Yes, hands-on." His smile
said he knew exactly what his touch meant.

Bud dropped something metal, making a
huge racket, but he wasn't looking at the
mess on the floor when she jerked her hand
back and glanced in his direction. No, he
was glaring at her. Well, actually, glaring at
Mike.

"How about we help you there, Bud?"
Mike asked as he scooted out of the booth.

"No. You take Josie on home in case Lisa
comes in early."

"It won't take long if you let us pitch in,"
Josie said.

"Naw. You two go on."

After they left the diner, Josie accepted
Mike's offer to follow her home. He walked
her to the porch, then loosely took hold of
her hands. He looked like a puppy dog waiting expectantly for a treat. Anyone who
thought of her as a treat . . . Well, she had
to like him. How could she not? He was so
earnest, so dedicated to Lisa. And there he
stood, looking as if he wanted to kiss her.

There was no way around the fact that she was starting to care for the guy. She had been since . . . Most likely since he'd tried to bear hug his niece that day while playing mini-golf.

Definitely since he'd talked to the woman at the boutique about buying her jewelry.

This guy could do serious damage to my heart. Especially since he and Lisa would leave soon. Their hug said they were ready to make their own way.

Do I want this badly enough, need this badly enough to risk it? Maybe Lisa's plan wasn't so crazy after all. At least temporarily.

"I had a really good time tonight," he said. "Thanks for showing me the town. And for the burger."

"I had fun, too. So I guess you aced Lesson Number Three." There was that look again. Was he going to kiss her? Did she even want him to? She wasn't certain she was ready.

"Lisa would be proud of me."

"Yeah. Who would have imagined it? Michael Throckmorton, Fun Guy."

He gave her hands a squeeze, then whispered, "It's Mike. I can be Mike when I'm with you."

CHAPTER ELEVEN

That night, Michael lay in bed with his arm thrown across his eyes, trying his best to get some rest. But he couldn't relax enough to go to sleep. He and Josie had shared a wonderful evening, and all was finally well with Lisa.

But he felt unsettled. Unsettled enough that he hadn't kissed Josie as he'd been tempted to do, as she'd looked as if she'd wanted. Unless maybe he'd imagined that part.

The trouble was, what now? Soon, he and Lisa would go back to Charleston. Soon, Josie would buy the diner, her life going on as planned.

But what was there for him in Charleston besides work? And for Lisa?

If, hypothetically, his parents didn't expect him to come back and take his place in the family business, would he choose to stay? As Josie had said, maybe it was time for him to consider God's plan.

Heavenly God, thank You for giving me this time to find Lisa. Thank You that she met Josie and that she's been safe. But now, Lord, I feel lost. I don't know where I belong. I'm torn between family responsibility and . . . and my calling? Or are they one and the same? Give me a calling, Lord. Please. And since I'm so new at this, I ask that You make it clear to me.

He pulled the blanket up and rolled over. *Extremely clear.*

His muscles relaxed and he began to drift, weightless, into darkness.

The ring of the phone jolted him straight up and sent his pulse pounding all over his body.

"Hello?"

"Don't panic," Josie said. "But Lisa's not back yet. I'm getting worried."

He ran his hand through his hair, trying to shake the fog out of his brain. The clock said midnight. "Okay. Let's see. How about I come over? We'll take it from there."

"Thank you," she said in a rush of breath. "See you in a minute."

He dressed and sped to Josie's house, every cell in his body now on full alert. What if she had run again? But surely not. She'd been cooperating so well the last day or so.

So if she wasn't running, could they have had car trouble? What if Brian was up to no good?

Or an accident.

He tried not to panic. He couldn't believe he'd been dumb enough to let her go out with a boy he didn't know. He didn't even know Brian's family.

When he arrived at Josie's, every light was on, inside and out. She met him on the porch with her arms out. He held her to him for a minute, then they went inside.

"Have you called Brian's house?" he asked.

"Yes. He's not there. But his curfew isn't until 1:00 a.m. They said they'd call if they heard from him."

Michael led Josie to the couch. He held her hand as they watched the clock tick off the minutes. Twelve forty-five rolled around, and he was physically sick to his stomach with worry.

He had to start thinking about the unthinkable. She could have been in an accident.

"I think we should call the police," he said. "And check with the hospitals."

"I agree."

As he was heading toward the phone, the sound of a car approaching drifted through the front windows. By the time they reached the door and slung it open, the car — which was actually a truck — sped away, leaving Lisa standing on the front sidewalk.

"Where have you been?" Michael barked.

Lisa stomped up the front walk. "Nowhere fun."

"Weren't you supposed to be at a movie?"

"We were. But it was terrible, so we left."

"Then where did you go?"

"A party at his friend's house."

Michael ground his teeth rather than spout off the smart remark that was on the tip of his tongue. "Get in the house right now."

"I'm not that late."

"You're over an hour late. We were about to call the hospitals." He took her by the arm. "I can't believe you didn't take five seconds to pick up a phone."

"Look, I'm sorry, okay? It's not the end of the world."

"You're grounded," he said much more calmly than he felt.

"You're kidding, right?"

"No. I've probably been too easy on you, not wanting to push you after your mother died. But it's time you acted more responsibly."

Considering he had just grounded her and

she was in major trouble, she didn't look too upset. Maybe she'd needed him to get firm with her sooner.

Josie stepped closer to them. "I guess you should head to bed, Lisa. You have to work early tomorrow."

"One question first," Michael said. "Why didn't Brian have the guts to walk you to the door to apologize?"

She stared at her feet. "Because he had been drinking."

Michael's heart nearly stopped. "Don't *ever* ride with someone who's had even a sip of alcohol. Do you understand me?"

"Yes, sir."

Josie was thrilled with the way Mike was handling the situation. He'd really stepped up to fill the role Lisa needed him to fill.

"Just to remind you," he added, "you're not to go anywhere unless it's to work or somewhere with Josie or me for a week."

"Not even the craft center?"

"No, and I'll give you two choices. You either abide by my rules for being grounded. Or you go back to Charleston with me tonight — to your school and their rules."

The second option sent a wave of ice along Josie's spine. *Please, Lord, no.*

Lisa looked frightened. "I'm not going anywhere tonight."

"Then you're grounded. I won't bend on this, Lisa."

"Okay," she said on a sigh. "Good night."

Mike looked shaken. His helpless expression drew Josie across the space between them.

He wrapped his arms tightly around her. "If she ever does something so stupid again, I don't know what I'll do."

"You'll deal with whatever you have to. You did great tonight."

"I may just lock her up until she's thirty."

Josie rubbed his back. "I'm proud of you for standing firm tonight. You may survive the teen years after all."

"I'll hold you to that." He backed away from her. "I should go. Tomorrow, provided everything checks out at the bank, I'm going to look into leasing one of the houses I've seen for rent nearby. I could use a kitchen and place to wash clothes."

Josie's stomach did a little leap at the thought. He was talking about a longer commitment to work with Lisa. "I think that's a great idea, Mike. Here, let me give you a spare key so you can check on her anytime you want." She dug in her junk drawer and fished the key chain out.

"I was thinking while we waited tonight. I may have her move in with me at the rental, but I need to consider that some more. Right now, it's good for her to have a female presence. Your presence."

Josie swallowed hard. "I'm glad I can be here for her."

"Promise you'll tell me if you get sick of dealing with us?"

She definitely didn't foresee that happening. "I promise. I'll give you a swift kick down the highway when I get tired of you."

He caressed her face with his big, strong hands, thumbs brushing over her cheeks as he stared at her mouth. But instead of kissing her, he pulled her to him, not so much a hug of desperation as before, but a tender, gentle embrace. Then he tightened his hold as if he sensed she was about to fall.

When he finally released her, he said, "Thank you for taking care of my family." Then he kissed her forehead and left.

Shaken more by the night's events than she cared to admit, Josie tiptoed to peek in Lisa's room. Lisa and Brian could have had a wreck. And what if he had tried to take advantage of her?

Lisa stirred, so Josie sat beside her on the bed. When she did, Josie heard purring, and found a warm, furry body snuggled up to Lisa's chest. Josie sighed but didn't mention the broken rule. "Are you okay?"

"Yeah. Just hoping I didn't blow it with Uncle Michael."

"Oh, I don't think so. He loves you no matter what." She smoothed Lisa's hair from her forehead. "Did Brian behave tonight?"

Lisa snorted a groggy laugh. "Even under the influence, Brian turned out to be a regular Michael Throckmorton. B-O-R-I-N-G." She rolled away from Josie and snuggled into her pillow.

Josie was surprised at how the urge to protect Mike nearly overwhelmed her. "Well, learn this lesson right now, Lisa — Michael Throckmorton is a good man, and any woman would be lucky to have him."

"And he'd be lucky to have you," she murmured as she appeared to drift off to sleep.

Deep breathing became light snores.

Josie battled tears all the way to the back door where she set the cat outside. Once she took an allergy pill, locked up and turned off the lights, she threw herself on her bed. Sobs ripped from her — the sobs she'd stored up from all those Hallmark commercials over the last twenty-nine years. But she couldn't hold them in any longer. Sure, any woman would be lucky to have Mike, but Josie would never be *the* lucky

woman. Because if she entered his life —
which was a joke; imagine her on his arm at
a chamber of commerce meeting — she
would drown.

Living in his rich, high-society world
would crush her spirit, just like living with a
domineering tyrant had crushed Josie's
mom's spirit.

Michael used the key and let himself into
Josie's house at seven the next morning.
Josie had left for work at six. As he'd
expected, she'd let Lisa sleep in.

Well, he wouldn't allow it. *Let her pay for
her antics.*

He banged on the bedroom door. "Lisa,
get up."

After a pitiful whine, she said, "No way."

"No choice. Get up now, or I'll come drag
you out."

"Pleeeease, let me sleep."

"By three. One . . ."

No sound.

"Two . . ."

This time he heard a couple of groans.

"Are you up?"

The door opened and a disheveled Lisa
squinted out at him.

"Go take a shower. You're going to work
today."

"But Uncle Michael . . ."

"You've got ten minutes."

"Fifteen."

"Ten."

She grumbled as she moved slowly toward the bathroom. Michael set his alarm on his watch for ten minutes and went to sit on the deck. He admired the wooded backyard and the crisp, clean air. He tried humming a few bars of Josie's praise song from the day before.

Was that only yesterday?

Today would be just as busy. He had to take Lisa to work, then he could look into renting a house. The one diagonally across the street would be perfect. And it still had a For Rent sign outside. Which reminded him he needed to call Gary.

He dialed Gary on his cell phone.

"Are you on your way home?" Gary asked in greeting.

"No. In fact, it's the opposite, I'm afraid. Lisa needs more time. And I'm thinking I'll stay longer, maybe rent a small place short-term."

"You're kidding, of course."

"No, Gar, I'm not."

Silence on the other end.

"Is something wrong with the Mason account?"

"No, it's fine. But Dad's not. He wants you back here ASAP, and I'm tired of hearing about it."

"I told him I have confidence in you."

"Well, he doesn't. I'm ready for you to get back here to keep him off my back."

"You know Lisa has to be my priority right now."

He sighed. "I know that. But it doesn't make life any easier for me and the other employees. You've given her time. Can't you make her come home now?"

"We had an incident last night. She drove with a kid who'd been drinking. I've grounded her."

"Then get her away from that kid. Carry out the punishment here at home."

"It's more complicated than that."

"You're going to have to be the grown-up here, Michael."

"Don't you see that's what I'm trying to do?" He realized he was yelling, so lowered his voice. "I'm staying until you hear otherwise. Let me know if you have any problems."

"Then you can be the one to tell Dad." Gary hung up without a goodbye.

Great, just what Michael needed. A headache first thing in the morning. He rubbed his temples.

How was he supposed to succeed if he didn't have the support of at least Gary?

Well, the call to his dad could wait.

He checked his watch. Lisa had another minute. Time for more prayer. He'd done nothing but pray since he'd left here last night. Nothing had ever terrified him as much as realizing Lisa could have been killed with Brian driving drunk.

Of course, it didn't matter now. Lisa wouldn't be allowed to see Brian again. She would be lucky to have another date during the next century.

Noises carried through the back door.

Dear God, be with me today as I have to carry out Lisa's grounding. And God, please keep her safe. Make her smart. Use this time to convince her to stay away from alcohol and from kids who drink it.

She opened the back door. "I'm ready."

His watch alarm sounded. "Wow, you're good."

"I need to feed the cat, then we can go."

"Josie mentioned a stray."

"Yeah, she showed up about the time I did. A scruffy, scrawny thing."

The cat must have heard Lisa pop the can open. It came running up the stairs onto the deck and rubbed against Lisa all the way to its dish. "Looks healthy now."

Lisa plopped the can of food into the bowl, then rubbed the cat. "She's beautiful after lots of TLC. I want to keep her, but Josie's allergic. So she's letting me feed her outside."

"Have you named her?"

"Not yet. I wasn't sure she'd stick around."

It hurt to hear the insecurity in her voice. "What about when you leave here?"

She shrugged, scratched behind the cat's ears. "Don't know."

One more issue to deal with when he and Lisa left Gatlinburg. "Let's get going."

Once she finished, they locked up and got in his car. She wouldn't look at him. He didn't force conversation at this point. He would save that for later, after she'd had time to think about her poor decision last night.

When they arrived at the diner, she tried to slink into the kitchen.

"Oh, no you don't. You're going to eat a good breakfast before you start your shift — which you will complete, by the way, even if you have to make up your missed breakfast hours another day."

She sighed.

"Here." He pointed at the table. "Josie, could you bring Lisa some breakfast, please?"

"Coming right up." She smiled, but it wasn't the warm greeting he'd expected. Well, he had Lisa to worry about right now.

Lisa slouched in the booth. "All I really need is coffee to help me wake up."

"You'll perk up with some food," he said.

Josie carried over a glass of orange juice and a glass of milk. Then she hurried over to the grill, where she scooped scrambled eggs onto a plate of fruit. She placed it in front of his niece. "Here you go, Lisa, honey. Did you get enough sleep?"

Lisa tried not to look at Michael accusingly, but he could see the frustration. "Yes, but I could use some caffeine. I'm sorry I'm late to work."

"It's okay. I let Bud know what happened." She patted Lisa on the shoulder. "Eat up." Then she hurried away to take another order.

Josie checked on Lisa occasionally, but she spent time between customers chatting with the construction guys. She didn't seem to want to talk this morning and seemed to be avoiding him. Surely she didn't think their embrace was a mistake. All he wanted was more of the same.

Maybe long-term.

What was he thinking? Because surely he

was crazy if he thought he and Josie could have some sort of relationship other than the time they had together right now.

Why not? Why can't we?

Because one of them would have to give up so much. She, her dream of owning the diner, and Bud. He, the bank and his family. Because his hypothetical situation — where his family didn't need him — would never happen.

"Uncle Michael, I'm sorry about last night. Really sorry."

He put his hand over Lisa's. "I forgive you. But do you understand how serious I am about not drinking and driving? We lost your mother that way. I don't want to lose you."

Tears welled up in her eyes. Her lip trembled. "You're right. I promise I'll be more careful. And responsible."

"Thank you." He sipped the coffee Josie had quietly brought him. After last night, he didn't want to tell Lisa he'd decided to have her live with him. Not until he was certain he'd made the right decision. Until he knew she would cooperate, that he would be able to keep her under control. And safe. "I've decided to stay around a little longer, to give you time to feel comfortable about leaving with me. I'm going to try to rent a house near Josie's."

"But your work . . ."

"As long as everything goes smoothly with your uncle Gary, I'll be fine staying with you a while longer."

"I guess I don't deserve this."

"Of course you do. You're my . . . niece. You're family. And I want to make sure you're ready to leave before we go back to Charleston." He patted her arm. "Now get to work before Bud fires you."

"Okay. I'll see you later."

"I'll tell you what. Josie's working a double today, so why don't we go hiking this afternoon?"

"Kind of like boot camp?"

He smiled at her. "Something like that."

Once Lisa had gone to the kitchen, Michael watched Josie as she continued to ignore him. Enough was enough. He wouldn't let her ignore what they'd shared. Even if it was only temporary.

He stalked toward her. "Excuse me." He tapped her on the shoulder. "Could we go for a quick walk?"

"No," Josie said. "I'm working."

"Bud," he called. "Could you spare Josie for a few minutes?"

She glared at Michael. "I can't —"

"That's up to Josie," Bud said. "But we

can do without her for a half hour now that Lisa is here."

Josie went with him grudgingly, only to keep from making a scene. Once outside and down the street a ways, she stopped dead in her tracks. "How dare you manhandle me into taking a break."

"I didn't —" He took her hands. "What's wrong, Josie?"

She snatched them back to her sides, trying to find the words to describe the horrible fear that had struck her last night after he'd left.

"Speechless, huh? That's a first," he teased.

"Okay. You asked for it." She stuffed some hair back up into her ponytail. "I'm freaking out over last night."

"Not over Lisa, I take it."

"Well, I freaked over that, too. But I'm talking about us. Me and you."

"Over one hug?"

"It was more than just a hug between friends, Mike, in case you didn't notice."

He stepped closer. "Believe me. I noticed."

She moved back the same distance he had moved forward. "You know good and well it was much more than a hug or holding hands. There seem to be feelings developing."

"That's funny. I sure couldn't tell by the way you were acting this morning."

She looked away, then forced herself to maintain eye contact. "I guess I've got 'morning after' guilt."

Laughter roared out of him. "I love your humor. And the way you tell it like it is."

Wasn't that just like him, to hit her right in the spot where she was vulnerable? The spot inside her that wanted to live loud and be allowed to be herself. She'd found a man who could appreciate those very qualities in her that had isolated her so many times.

The temptation to launch herself into his arms was like jet engines strapped to her feet.

He'll be a different person in Charleston.

Yep. Put him back in the bank, in the community, in his family, and he'd be the same man who'd walked into the diner exactly one week before.

No one changed that much in one week. Not for good anyway.

"Mike, you're only fascinated with me because I'm different from the women you've typically dated."

"You can say that again."

She laughed even though she didn't want to. "See, you're learning to speak your mind, too."

"I admit it is kind of nice. Can you teach me more?"

"You want to be a big mouth?"

"I want to be spontaneous." He pulled her closer. "Teach me to have more fun, Josie. I enjoyed last night so much."

As long as he was going to be in town, she could do that for him. Couldn't she?

Hard as it was, she managed to push him away. "Sure. Lisa and I can teach you to have fun." But she wouldn't let her heart get involved. She couldn't afford to.

They could make it work. As long as she could forget any crazy notions she'd had for long-term. They could enjoy each other's company and then say goodbye.

Michael spent the morning filling out a three-month lease agreement, the minimum he could get. But even if he only needed it a week, it would be worth every penny. He could afford to take the loss.

He then went about securing enough furniture to survive for a short while and buying a few groceries. Luckily, the house near Josie had all the appliances he would need — refrigerator and washer and dryer. The range would probably be an untouched bonus. Wal-Mart provided a microwave, linens, paper products, cleaning products and toiletries.

He felt as if he were setting up a college dorm room.

By the time he got sheets put on the bed — straight out of the package and as stiff as a nicely starched shirt — he barely made it on time to pick up Lisa.

She fell asleep in the car during the short drive to Josie's house. He woke her as he passed his new house.

"Lisa, wake up. I want to show you something."

She opened her eyes, but appeared addled. "What is it?"

"That house right there." He pointed. "I rented it today. I'll get you a key."

"Oh, okay. Am I going to live there, too?"

He couldn't tell whether she wanted to or not. "You're going to stay with Josie for now. But if you decide you'd like to move across the street, just let me know. We might be able to work something out."

She rubbed her hand over her eyes. "I'm cool with that."

Once they were at Josie's house, Lisa went to wash her face and change clothes. When she came out, she looked young and scrubbed clean, like a kid right out of the bathtub.

"So are you ready to hit the national

park?" he asked.

"Sure. And I'll even give you time to buy some boots this time."

Michael's new heavy-duty hiking boots squeezed his toes a tad, but he felt prepared for anything.

Lisa eyed her own new boots. "Thanks, again, Uncle Michael. I've wanted some like these for a long time."

"You're welcome." The most amazing part to him was that she'd had him buy himself a pair that matched hers.

He locked the car and slung the new backpack over his shoulder.

"You're such a Boy Scout." Lisa snorted a laugh. "A ton of supplies for a measly hike on a trail blazed by tourists of every age."

"Hey, my motto really is to be prepared." Especially when alone with his niece who would most likely blaze her own trails throughout life.

Just like Josie.

He had to laugh at his lack of preparedness when it came to Josie, though. Including his failure to protect his heart.

He and Lisa headed up the worn path not far behind some other hikers. But it didn't take five minutes for Lisa to point the way down a rocky slope. "These boots are made for hiking," she sang. "Not meandering."

With no other choice, he started out after her. "Okay. At least I brought my cell phone in case we get lost."

"Good luck getting a signal."

They made their way through overgrown vines and underbrush. He followed her, checking a compass every so often.

"Oh, good. There's a stream up ahead," she said. "I'm getting a blister on my heel."

"And I, the Boy Scout, have a bandage."

"I guess I'll have to quit teasing you if you'll give me one."

He sat on the grassy incline and watched her peel off one boot and sock, then stick that foot into the icy water.

It was hard to believe this was the same girl who had hiked at the river only days before.

She smiled at him and his heart lurched. "You look so much like your mom," he said.

She lifted her foot out of the water and stood on the other like a stork. "Do I really? 'Cause she was, like, really pretty in old pictures."

"She was really pretty. And so are you."

Lisa stood on both legs once again. "Tell me something about her. Something good."

The good memories were so buried in the more recent bad memories that it took him a minute to reprogram his musings.

Forget the alcohol and drugs, Michael. Find Patricia.

Suddenly, he had a picture form in his mind. "Your mom loved dolls. Especially one baby she got when she was about five or six. She got new ones through the years, but none ever compared to that worn, ratty-haired one." He tossed a rock into the stream. "She took such good care of it. I couldn't figure out how she learned. Your grandmother was never very maternal."

"Maybe she treated the doll like she always wished Grandmother would treat her."

"I suppose you're right." He unzipped his pack to get a bandage for her blister.

"What was the doll's name?" She peeled off the paper and applied it to her heel.

He recalled Patricia putting the baby in a toy high chair and feeding it. What was it she'd called the thing? She'd rocked the doll and sung to it, calling it — The name hit him like a kick in the gut.

"Lisa," he choked out. "She called her Lisa."

Tears puddled in his niece's eyes but didn't spill over. She put her sock and boot back on and started to climb on the rocks. "Thanks for telling me, Uncle Michael."

"Any time. I'd be happy to tell you anything you want to know."

"Come on, old man. You need to test out those boots." She hopped to a nearby rock, landing easily with perfect traction. "They're great!"

He eased onto a rock near the edge of the water, scuffing his sole back and forth, testing the treads. "They do hold pretty well." He leaped out to a rock beside the one she was on.

The air was nippy, but the sun shone brightly, lighting her rosy cheeks. She was the picture of wholesomeness — if he could imagine her with brown hair instead of green.

He could do this. He could take her home and form a two-person family. How hard could it be? Josie had prepared him well. He could take Lisa shopping. Even if he couldn't cook much, he could take her to restaurants. They could have fun together playing golf, hiking, maybe going to movies or whatever else teens liked to do.

He could even ground her when it was necessary to discipline her.

This wasn't so hard after all, as long as he was willing to try new things. To be more spontaneous.

"Come on, Uncle Michael. I'll race you

across the stream. Last one there buys pizza for dinner."

"I don't know. Maybe if we take it slow."

"Ready, set, go," she yelled, then took off.

The boots did grip well. And she was getting ahead.

He jumped to a nearby rock, hoping to find a shortcut from the path she seemed to be taking. Once he landed, he saw the perfect sequence. He quickly pulled ahead of her. "I've got it now. You'll never win."

"You're dreaming." She laughed. He could hear her huffing behind him, drawing closer. She squealed.

His heart pounded from the strain. He'd been holding his breath each time he leaped. He took a deep breath and made the last lunge toward land. With his arms in the air, he turned to celebrate his victory and rub it in.

She was gone.

He searched, his lungs feeling as if they might burst out of his chest.

He saw her lying on her back in the water, her face barely above the surface. "Please God, no."

CHAPTER TWELVE

Michael ran to Lisa, splashing in water over his ankles. When he reached her, he knelt and gently felt for a heartbeat. She had a pulse, and was breathing, but she was unconscious. A quick search showed blood oozing from a wound on the back of her head.

She must have fallen backward and hit her head on a rock.

He yanked out his cell phone and dialed 9-1-1, praising God that he had one bar of signal. After giving approximate directions to where they were, he followed the dispatcher's instructions to carefully move her out of the frigid water while trying to stabilize her neck.

Gently, he carried her to the grass. Once she was bundled under his coat, he applied pressure to her wound with sterile gauze out of his first-aid kit.

She opened her eyes. "Uncle Michael?"

"Yeah, honey. I'm here. You must've fallen."

"Did I win?"

A laugh worked its way through the fear and panic. "You sure did. I'm buying tonight."

"I don't think I feel like eating pizza." She heaved herself up and lost her lunch on the ground.

At least her back and neck weren't injured. But she needed to get to a hospital to be checked for a concussion. And maybe stitches. "Come on, honey. Hold this gauze against your head, and I'll carry you up to the car. There should be an ambulance soon."

"Okay." She looked pale. And in pain.

What had he been thinking, racing across slippery rocks? Why had he ever thought he could take care of someone?

Josie shuffled into the house, thankful Regina had made it to the diner so she didn't have to work a full double, but still worn out. All she wanted was a hot shower and to wash the grease out of her hair.

Once she'd indulged, she came out fresh and peachy. While toweling her curls to absorb the excess water, she went to the kitchen to get a glass of iced tea. The flash of the answering machine caught her attention. She didn't get many messages, so she pushed the button.

"Josie, it's Michael. Lisa's had an accident."

The blood rushed from Josie's face leaving her light-headed.

"We're on our way to the hospital to have her checked. I'll try you at the diner."

The machine clicked off. No other messages.

"Mike! Which hospital?"

Paralyzed with fear, Josie's brain had to kick into gear and make her body start moving. *First shoes. Then call the closest hospital to see if they're there.*

Ice froze Josie's insides as she grabbed the phone book, her leaden hands almost too stiff to turn the pages. Once she found the listing of the nearest hospital, she punched in the number.

"Emergency room."

"Could you tell me if you've had a Lisa Throckmorton admitted?"

"Hold, please."

Josie gripped the phone cord to her chest. *Please, God.*

"Yes, I see a Throckmorton came in around a half hour ago."

Josie swallowed, almost unable to speak.

"Can . . . can you tell me what happened? What her condition is?"

"I'm sorry, unless you're a member of the immediate family, I can't give out that information."

Josie fought tears as she realized how much Mike and Lisa meant to her. "Look, lady. They're the only family I have."

"Oh, I'm sorry, Mrs. Throckmorton. All I know at the moment is that it's a head injury, and she's gone for a CT scan."

Oh, dear Lord. A head injury? "Thank you." Josie slammed down the phone, grabbed her keys and ran out to her car. She raced to the hospital emergency entrance and parked among the ambulances.

Mike had left her name at the reception desk. They led her through a set of double doors to an examination room. She barreled in and saw Lisa lying on a stretcher with a bandage around her head. "What happened?"

Mike startled. "Shh. You're going to hurt her head banging around like that."

"Tell me what happened. Is she okay?"

He took Josie's hand and led her to the bed. "We were in the park, and she slipped on a rock in the stream. Has a concussion. But she's going to be fine."

Tears gushed out of Josie's eyes as she

started to shake all over. "I got home . . . Your message . . . I was so scared."

"It's just a stupid bump on the head and a few stitches," Lisa muttered. "It's not like they had to take a kidney or somethin'."

Tears of relief mingled with the tears of fright. Then Josie started laughing.

"Do you do a lot of that?" Mike smiled at her. "That laughing and crying at the same time?"

"Only since I realized I love this green-headed renegade." She looked at Lisa and tried to smile through wobbly lips.

."I love you, too, Josie." Lisa's face crumpled. Tears welled up and she started to cry. Then she, too, ended up laughing. "Ouch. That hurts. Stop it, Josie."

When Josie let out a hysterical laugh-wail, Lisa laughed harder. Which led to a pain-filled groan from the patient. "Oh, that hurts."

"Are you two going to be okay, now?" Mike asked.

Lisa passed the tissue box to Josie, who took one, wiped her eyes, then blew her nose with a loud honk.

Lisa swiped at her tears. "I know I don't show it. But I love you, Uncle Mike."

"Uncle Mike?" he said, unsure of how to answer her. He'd never told anyone he loved them before, not even Gloria. And he couldn't remember anyone telling him, either.

"Yeah," Lisa said. "I think you've earned the nickname."

Michael reached for his niece. Maybe it wasn't possible to plan for moments like this. Maybe you just had to go for it. "You know, I love you, too. From the minute I first saw you bundled in a pink hospital blanket." He caressed her face.

"Ouch," Lisa said.

He jerked his hand away. "Did I hurt you?"

"It's okay. Like I said, it's —" she took in several puffs of air "— it's only a stupid —" tears spurted out of the corners of her eyes "— bump on the head." She began to sob.

He leaned over to comfort her, trying not to cause any pain. He patted Lisa's hand, a safe area. "What's wrong, pumpkin?"

"Pumpkin? No one's called me that in . . . so . . . loooong." The wailing began in earnest, then.

Michael glanced up at a crying Josie. His eyes were the only dry ones in the room, but they prickled, on the verge.

Trying to lighten the moment, he said to Lisa, "Hey, don't cry. Your hair will grow back and the scar won't show."

"I can just shave the rest of it off," Lisa said, attempting to smile but failing.

"Over my dead body."

Josie playfully slapped Michael away and took Lisa's hand. "Are you okay? Really okay?"

"I'm better than okay." She sniffed. "Even though my head hurts, I'm happy. This is just what I prayed for."

Michael grinned. "You prayed that we'd be around your hospital bed crying?"

"No, goofball. I prayed that we'd be, like, you know . . . a family."

Michael saw the doubt in Josie's dazed expression. And maybe a little fear?

He knew the feeling. Seeing each other temporarily and marrying, forming a family, were two totally different things. He wasn't sure he'd ever be ready to take on *that* commitment.

Then again, God was omnipotent.

Michael looked at his niece. "What *exactly* did you pray for?"

Once Lisa was resting peacefully, Michael asked Josie to sit with her. He needed to call his family and let them know about the accident.

As he walked outside the hospital, he thought about all the panic and fear of the last two days. He'd had to deal with Lisa staying out past curfew, and now the concussion. Were teenagers always this much trouble?

Whether they were or not didn't matter. What mattered was that he apparently wasn't parent material. If he couldn't protect Lisa from herself, how was he supposed to protect her from the world?

He opened his cell phone and dialed Gary.

"Hey, Michael. What's up?"

"We're at the hospital with Lisa. She's had a little accident. Slipped and fell and has a concussion."

"Oh, no. Is she okay?"

"Had to get some stitches. We'll have to watch her tonight."

"I'll drive up there to check on her tomorrow. I'll see if I can get someone to cover for me at the bank on Monday morning."

"You don't have to do that."

"I want to. And I'll let Mother and Dad know."

"Thanks, Gary."

"I, uh . . ." He paused on the other end of the line. "I was about to call you, anyway."

"What's up?"

"Tom Mason is having second thoughts."

Michael had to shift gears from Lisa to business. Alarm at the tone of Gary's voice made for a rapid transition. "But he signed the contract. The financing is lined up."

"We only shook on it. We were going to sign the paperwork today."

"Then what's the problem?"

"I guess he's figured out I'm new at all this. He wants to sit down and go over the contract with you."

"I can't, Gar. You were the one to win him over. Act confident, and he'll come around."

"I tried that. When it comes to dinner and golf, I'm the man. But when it comes to contracts, your reputation and experience make you the man."

"Can you put him off a couple of weeks?"

"He's got construction deadlines to meet. He said he could wait until Monday, but that's it."

"Did you suggest Dad?"

"He won't hear of it. Seems they've had conflicts before."

This couldn't be happening. Michael wanted to get all of Mason's business so badly he could taste it. It could make the difference between an okay year and a great year dividend-wise. They only had a few stockholders outside the family, but he had a responsibility to them.

Since Lisa was going to be laid up for a day or two, maybe he could make the trip to Charleston.

But what if she needs me while I'm gone?

Josie could take care of any situation, couldn't she?

"Michael, I really need you here ASAP."

"Let me call him."

"I suggested a conference call. He said he wouldn't consider talking through a contract on the phone."

"Can he meet me here? We could fly him."

"I've tried everything, big brother. He can't get away right now."

So after all the months of work, it came down to choosing Lisa or Tom Mason.

Michael walked farther into the parking lot. He could see Josie's car parked haphazardly in a no-parking area. He pictured taking Lisa back to Josie's house. Lisa would walk in the door and drop her things, then throw herself into their arms and say, "I love you both."

"I'm sorry, Gary. Lisa needs me right now."

Silence. Then a big sigh. "Just think about it. Once I get there, maybe I can stay with Lisa while you head home to deal with Mason."

"Okay. I'll see how she's doing once you get here."

"I'm sorry, Michael. I know how hard

you've worked for this account."

Shoving his frustration and disappointment aside, he said, "Hey, you did a great job. The contract experience will come."

"I should definitely cut my teeth on smaller fish."

Michael laughed. "That's a plan."

"I do wish you were back at the bank, but I'm glad Lisa has you there for her now. She's needed you the whole time, you know."

"Yeah. I'm learning the hard way, too."

It was late when the hospital finally released Lisa into Michael's care. As he helped load her into his car, Lisa said, "Thanks for taking such good care of me today, Uncle Mike."

"Good care of you? Don't forget I'm the idiot who raced you across the rocks."

She shrugged. "I would have done it with or without you. And, hey, at least you had your first-aid kit. I'll never again make fun of you for being overly prepared."

How could she be so forgiving? She should be blaming him.

"She's right, Mike," Josie said. "Accidents are going to happen. And you handled it well."

"Handled it well? I thought my heart

would explode, it was pounding so fast."

"But you kept a level head. Told the paramedics where to find you. Stopped the blood flow."

"How did you know all that?" he asked.

"The nurses were bragging on you," Lisa said. "And were drooling over you." She rolled her eyes.

Having someone — two someones — believe in you was a heady thing. Even though he didn't deserve it, he basked in their praise.

Maybe, just maybe, with God's help, he would be able to take care of Lisa.

Once they arrived at Josie's, they decided she would watch Lisa overnight for practical reasons. He helped them get settled, then went home and fell into bed. He and Josie had prayed together for Lisa, and it had certainly helped calm him. But he missed the sound of the river rushing outside his motel room. Except for a few creaks, his new little house was too quiet to lull him to sleep at night.

So sleep eluded him. And when it did come, visions of Lisa in the basket of a bike, riding across the sky with Toto, haunted his dreams. He woke several times tangled in the sheets, thinking a house had fallen on him.

Somewhere before dawn, he finally gave up and decided that going for a run might rejuvenate him. He got out of bed, put on his running clothes, then hopped in his car and drove the streets around his house to measure a route. Once he had three-point-two miles mapped out, he went for the morning run he had missed on Friday while dealing with Lisa's grounding.

He found the hills made it harder than he'd expected, and could only do about two miles. But the change in routine didn't bother him as it once would have. He couldn't wait to tell Josie the news.

When he returned, it was still too early to head over to Josie's. He puttered around the house, imagining what it would be like to work from his home in Charleston. He could probably do a third of his work by telecommuting. Gary could take on more responsibility. Michael could drop quite a few civic positions. And he was on too many corporate boards. Rotating off those would cut down on travel.

Michael could go in to the bank while Lisa was at school. He could leave when it was time for her to come home, could work there in the afternoons. The plan truly had merit, and the more he thought about it, the more he liked it. He was surprisingly excited about getting back to work.

If he made those changes, he could let her live with him and go to a nearby school. Maybe she would feel as if she fit in better at a public school.

Considering so many changes shot his blood pressure up a few notches, but not sky-high the way it would have a week earlier. Thanks to Josie, he was more competent.

Thanks to Josie, he now knew what his priorities were.

But it would all be a balancing act. He still had to decide what to do about going back to meet with Tom Mason.

And what about Josie? Where would she fit in the picture?

CHAPTER THIRTEEN

Josie had had a rough night. She was supposed to have roused Lisa every two hours. But instead, she'd poked and prodded the patient every few minutes all night long, scared to let her sleep at all. So, Josie wasn't in the best of moods when Mike showed up at seven that morning.

"How's the patient?"

Too exhausted to talk, she pointed him toward Lisa's room.

When he returned, he said, "Go to bed. I'll watch her now."

He didn't have to tell her twice. She crawled off to bed to get some real sleep.

She woke two hours later, showered, then got dressed for church. While Mike was waking Lisa, the doorbell rang. Josie opened the door to find Officer Fredrickson and his wife, along with Bud and Regina. "Hi, come in."

"I was at Bud's yesterday when Michael

called looking for you," Regina said. "How's Lisa?"

"I'd be fine if Josie hadn't kept waking me up all night," the patient said as she walked out of her room, rubbing sleep from her eyes.

"We knew you were at the hospital late. Brought breakfast," Bud said. He directed everyone to the kitchen while Josie introduced Mrs. Fredrickson to Mike and Lisa.

"We sure were worried," Officer Fredrickson said as his wife helped Bud set up the food.

"It gave me a good scare," Mike said. "Until she woke and asked if she'd won the race across the rocks."

"He said I won. I got stitches. You wanna see 'em?"

"Not right now, Lisa. We need to eat so we can get to church on time. I hope you'll all stay to share this wonderful meal you brought." Josie looked at Bud. "And to go to church with us."

She'd invited him hundreds of times over the years. Never once had he accepted. She didn't expect him to now.

"Come on, Bud. You've got to hear Josie belt out the songs. It's totally embarrassing." Lisa grinned at Josie, then gently rubbed her bandage.

247

Bud studied the pan of his famous cinnamon rolls as he took off the foil. "Well, now, I'm not sure I can resist that sight."

Regina's eyebrows raised in surprise. She, too, had been working on Bud.

"Then let's all eat and caravan over to the church," Mike said. He touched Josie's arm, giving it a little squeeze, then smiled at her. Apparently, he understood how much the acceptance meant to her.

"All those with sewn-up heads get to be first in line!" Lisa said as she began to pile food on her plate.

It had been ages since Josie had had people over for a meal. Granted, breakfast was a bit unusual. But it was nice to know she had such good, caring friends.

And that Bud would finally attend church with her.

Thank you, Lord, for working this miracle.

Before making her plate, Josie slipped over to the counter where her purse sat by the phone. She pulled out all the change she could dig up from her wallet and the bottom of her bag.

"Let me," Lisa whispered. She took the change from Josie and dropped it in the thankful box.

They attended the morning worship service

together. Lisa went without a fuss since she had the novelty of Bud along. She also wore clothes Mike approved of.

Bud acted nervous at first, but eventually relaxed enough to meet some of the members. He even said he would like to attend the following week. Josie couldn't have been happier.

After they dropped him and Regina off at the diner and arrived at home, Lisa went back to her room to supposedly rest. The house was comfortably silent, with just the faint sound of Lisa talking to her uncle Gary on the phone.

Josie forced herself to balance the checkbook. Mike sat at her computer desk, checking e-mails.

Lisa clanged the phone down. "It's too *quiet* out there. Shouldn't I hear kissing or something?"

"Quit goofing around and go to sleep," Mike called back.

Josie walked to Lisa's bedroom. "You need some uninterrupted rest."

"I'm not an invalid."

"I guess you could clean the house."

"Night, night."

Josie winked at Lisa and pulled the door closed.

She returned to one end of the couch and

snuggled under a blanket, then studied Mike at the computer. She could tell by his expression that he was working, not writing personal e-mails. His brow furrowed, and he had a near-frown on his face. For a moment, his typing became very brisk, and he punched at the keys as if angry.

"I wouldn't want to be the object of your wrath," she said.

"It's a couple of employees who can't get along. Petty arguing infuriates me."

She could relate. She'd seen it at the diner.

"How do you feel when you're at work?" she asked.

"Busy. Rushed."

"No, I mean your feelings. Personal."

He clicked a few more keys, then got up from the computer. He joined her on the couch, at the opposite end. Not too close. But not across the room in a chair.

He sighed. "Frustrated."

"That's more what I'm talking about."

After a pause, as if thinking, he said, "Uneasy. Almost as if I'm waiting for something bad to happen." He laughed. "I never realized that before."

"Do you get along with your dad and Gary at work?"

"Gary's fine. Dad, well, I guess we get along okay. I've found I dread when he shows up at my office, though. There's usually something wrong, some mess I have to straighten out."

"Sounds stressful."

"Believe it or not, it is. But there's a lot of the job I enjoy."

"So you'll be the top dog when your dad retires someday?"

"That's been the plan."

"Whose plan?"

He raised his brows at her. "My plan."

She raised her eyebrows, questioning his answer.

"And my parents' plan. But it truly has been mine as well. Mainly because I've never considered anything else."

"What about now? With Lisa and all," she quickly added, afraid he would think she was asking in regard to herself.

"I have some ideas of how it might work. Need to do more thinking, though."

"You'll figure out what you want to do, Mike. Keep praying about it."

"How long have you had your plan to buy the diner?"

"I've always wanted to have my own business, to be my own boss. It's been my dream since I was seven and opened a root-beer stand."

"Root beer?"

"I hated lemonade."

He chuckled. "I see. Well, I'm sure you'll be successful." He started to stand, then sat back down, looking as if he wanted to say something.

"What?"

"I can help you buy it sooner, you know. With financial backing."

"Absolutely not."

"Be practical, Josie. With a waitress's salary and tips, it'll take much longer."

"It's my dream. I can handle it."

"You're just being stubborn. If I'm in a position to help, why not let me?"

"Because then I'll feel like I have to run my business the way you want me to. It defeats the purpose of being in charge of my life, of succeeding on my own. Besides, it won't be much longer."

"I'm talking about a business partnership. We'd be equal. I wouldn't tell you what to do."

Why did the thought of a business partnership depress her? Because she was hopeful for another type of partnership?

She had a sudden craving to know every little detail about him. To find out what made him tick. "What about you, Mike? What's your dream? Not your plan. But your dream."

A flicker of sadness crossed his features. He started to speak, then hesitated. "Honestly?"

"Of course."

"I have no idea. Since I've been here, I've realized I never let myself dream."

"How sad."

"That's changing though, thanks to you. And to Lisa. But I still have a duty to my family. My job is more than just business."

Yeah, and she could just imagine what his family would think of her inserting herself into their plan for Mike. She would be their worst nightmare for their eldest, their pride and joy.

She would never fit into his high-society life. And she didn't want to try.

But would he ever consider fitting into her world?

He scooted closer to her, then took her hand. He brushed his thumb over her knuckles. "I have to focus on Lisa right now, you know."

"Of course. That's what I want."

"I can't look too far ahead. I'm trying to take one day at a time."

"Yeah, me, too." His touch sent her heart racing, but his words sent her stomach plummeting. Was he trying to give her the brush-off?

"I can't see how everything will work out. But I want you to know I care for you. And I've asked God to give me direction."

"I hope He does," she said stupidly, unsure how to handle his admission.

"I know I sound indecisive. Believe me, it's a first, and it's driving me crazy."

She nodded, unable to form words — probably a first for her, too.

"But I hope you'll trust me, that I want what's best for everyone."

"I do trust you." *I think. Maybe. But maybe not.* She faced him and gazed into his serious, so-tempting eyes. This man made her want to trust. More than any other man had before.

He grinned, a lazy, confident grin. "I'm not so sure you do. But that's okay for now. I plan to prove myself eventually. With God's help."

What could God have planned? Was there some way He could work out a way for Mike and her to be together?

It would require a miracle, because Josie couldn't begin to imagine a way for it to be possible.

Josie made an excuse to dash off to the grocery store after their conversation. She was getting way too cozy and falling under his spell. She had to be stronger or she'd be a goner, lost to him just as her mother had lost herself to Josie's dad.

Mike sent her to the store in his car with his cell phone. He was afraid her car would break down and leave her stranded somewhere. As if she hadn't been perfectly safe for all the years before he'd shown up.

See, he's being overbearing already.

He cares about you, a little voice in the back of her mind tried to tell her. But she wasn't buying it. He would suck her in with his caring and talk of trust. But she knew he was just caught up in the moment, in the sparks that flashed between them. When it came to introducing her to his family, he would bow out gracefully.

She was sure of the gracefully part. His breeding would demand it.

For the first time in years, she wanted to call her parents, to see if maybe her mom could offer some wisdom. Josie felt cheated at not having a woman she could count on over the years. Maybe it was time to forgive past hurts and see if her mom had changed.

Maybe her dad had even mellowed by now.

She pulled into the parking lot at a nearby market, making sure to park as far as possible from any other car. She was a nervous wreck driving a car that cost more than she made in three years, tips included.

Mike's cell phone beckoned. Did she even remember her old phone number?

The numbers sailed through her mind in perfect sequence as if she'd been dialing them every day for the past twelve years.

In all honesty, she'd thought about calling probably once a week, every week, for all those years. Which came out to . . . 624 almost-phone-calls.

Had Mom and Dad ever once picked up the phone to try to locate her?

That didn't matter. What mattered was that she do what God had been urging her to do. To forgive them and make an attempt at healing.

Her fingers flew over the buttons; the phone rang once, twice, three —

"Hello?" a woman said.

"Mom?"

Silence.

"Is this still the Miller residence?" A sudden sob closed her throat.

"Josephine, is that you?"

"Yeah, Mom. It's me." She swallowed back the runaway emotion. "How are you?"

"Oh, honey, it's so good —" she paused as if trying to compose herself, as well "—

so good to hear from you. Is everything okay?"

"I'm fine, Mom. I'm living in Gatlinburg now."

"I know. Do you like it there?"

"How did you know where I am?"

"We've kept up through your friends."

They had? Why hadn't they ever tried to contact her? "I just felt, well, like talking to you. To find out how you're doing."

"We're doing just fine, baby. Your dad's not here right now."

"He's working?"

"No. He's playing golf at the club. I'm about to go over there for a charity auction I'm coordinating."

"What charity?"

"A child advocacy program. We work with children in the foster-care system."

Her mother was working with children? "That's great, Mom. I'm proud of you."

They sat through an awkward silence.

"Well, honey, I hate to, but I really should go. I'm running late, and the kids are counting on me."

Yeah, like I couldn't ever do.

No, that wasn't fair. Josie had been a difficult child. And she'd run off, never giving them a chance.

But there was no way Josie would ever let

Lisa down like that. If she ever got the chance, that was.

"It was good talking to you, Mom."

"I'm glad you called. I hope you'll call back when your dad's home. He'll be sorry he missed you."

Yeah, right.

Quit whining and do what you planned to do.

"Mom, I'm sorry for the hurt I must've caused when I ran away."

"I — I'm sorry, too. I failed you somehow."

She had, but it would be cruel to say so. "No. I just had to find myself." Josie laughed at how trite that sounded. "I'm fine, now. I'm working toward buying a small diner. And I — I need to be quiet and let you go. I'll call back another time when we can talk."

"I'm sorry, Josephine. I really *must* run now. I'll look forward to your call."

"Sure, Mom. Bye."

The emptiness that had lived inside Josie since running away exploded out of the small corner she had shoved it into and bloomed into a huge, aching thing.

How could she possibly trust Mike with a need so overpowering? If she did, and he failed her, she might just bleed to death.

Josie returned with a loaf of bread and a chip on her shoulder the size of Texas.

"What happened at the store that's made you such a grump?" Michael asked.

"It could be the fact that she terrorized me all night," Lisa said. "She demanded to know the date, my name and the current president."

He could tell it was more than that. Something had happened. "Did you wreck my car? Is that what's bothering you?"

"So what if I did? Would you shoot me for damaging your *luxury* sedan?"

She said *luxury* with such a sneer that it hit him like a slap in the face. "No, I would simply let insurance take care of it."

"Or you'd just fork out another seventy grand for a new one. No big deal."

"I'm outta here," Lisa said. "You two can work this puppy out by yourselves."

Josie marched into the kitchen.

Michael followed. She slammed the bread into an antique bread keeper. One of the door hinges snapped at the force, causing it to list to the side.

"No need to tear up your antiques," he said.

"It's not an antique. It's a piece of junk I bought at an estate sale."

"Someone loved it enough to keep it all those years."

She reached for the hinge and tried to work it back in place, but a piece clanked onto the countertop.

Josie's head drooped. Her shoulders shook. "You're right. Someone loved it. And I ruined it." Tears choked her words.

He turned her around and held her in his arms, letting her cry. "What happened this afternoon?"

"I called home."

No wonder. "How did it go?"

She sniffed. "Okay. But my mother couldn't talk long. She's spearheading a charity auction for kids and didn't want to be late."

Ouch. Couldn't the woman have refrained from giving that piece of information so soon? "I'm sure she was relieved to hear from you."

"She knew where I was all along. They've kept tabs on me through supposed friends."

"And they never contacted you?"

"Not once." She pulled away and jerked off a square of paper towel, then proceeded to blow her nose on the stiff, rough paper. "But I never once called them, either." She tossed the wadded towel into the trash can. "I know I sound like a baby. It shouldn't matter anymore."

"It always matters when it's your parents." Which was why he was in such a quandary about what to do with his position at the bank — his position in the family, ultimately, because the bank was their life.

She attempted a pitiful smile. "Well, I did what I set out to do. I apologized for hurting them by running away." She laughed. "It doesn't look like I did much damage."

"I'm sure it hurt them. They did what they had to do to move on."

"Yeah, well . . . I need a nap."

"Good idea."

"Will you stay and watch Lisa while I rest?"

"Sure." He wanted, somehow, to offer comfort, and reached out to touch her cheek. But she turned her face away. He dropped his hand to his side. "Sleep well."

Michael and Lisa opened the front door to let in the warm afternoon breeze and played a competitive game of Monopoly on the coffee table. It was the perfect distraction from his worry about Josie.

Two hours later, he and Lisa were still battling it out.

"You better pay up on the hotel rental, Uncle Mike."

Lisa played a *viciously* competitive game. "You have no mercy."

"I bet you're the same when someone comes in for a loan."

"Hey, no fair. It's a business."

"Well, I'm, like, the queen of my hotel business. And I say I won't loan you any more money to pay your rent. You owe me . . ." She checked her sheet of scrap paper. "Two hundred thirty-three thousand four hundred and six dollars."

"No interest? You're a poor business-woman."

"But she's learning from the best," a voice — Gary's — said from the front porch.

"Uncle Gary!" Lisa hopped up and ran to him. They hugged, and once again, Michael marveled at Gary's easiness with Lisa. It was a shame that he'd been almost as ir-responsible as Patricia until her death. He was just now getting his life together and trying to make his way at the bank. Other-wise, he would have made a good guardian.

"Let's see that cracked noggin," Gary said to Lisa.

She proudly showed him her bandage. "I can show you the stitches later when we change the gauze."

"I'd like to see."

"How'd you get here so fast?" Lisa asked.

"Michael called me from the hospital. When I talked to you on the phone this morning, I was already on the way here. I had to come see you for myself to make sure you're okay."

"Why didn't Grandmother and Grandfather come?"

"They couldn't come today. But they were so worried they're going to try to come tomorrow."

Michael wished Gary hadn't mentioned them. He was afraid they wouldn't show now that they knew Lisa was doing well, and that she would feel let down.

"Oh, okay," Lisa said. "Hey, the ride to the hospital in the ambulance was pretty cool. Except, I guess getting knocked out messed up my brain a little. I don't really remember them putting me in."

It was the first she'd spoken of the trip to the hospital, and knowing she had been so vulnerable sent the pit of Michael's stomach into a free fall.

Instead of dwelling on it, he got up and shook hands with Gary. "I hope you're staying the night."

"I wouldn't miss seeing your rental house."

Gary smiled and Michael realized how much he'd missed his brother. "It's good to see you, Gar."

"Same here."

The handshake turned into a quick rough hug and a firm pat on the back. It was probably the most affection they'd ever shown each other.

"So, this is where you've been staying," Gary said to Lisa.

"Yeah. You'll have to meet Josie. She's sleeping right now."

"Oh. Okay."

"She was up with Lisa all night," Michael felt compelled to add.

"They couldn't let me get into a deep sleep, or I might have died." The excitement of the horrible episode brightened Lisa's expression. "Josie was scared I'd croak, so she woke me up about a gazillion times. Drove me insane."

Gary looked at Michael. "Sounds like this Josie's taking real good care of you."

Is he talking to Lisa or to me?

"Yes, she's a fine nurse," Michael said.

Lisa snorted a laugh. "She's more than that, Uncle Mike."

"Uncle Mike?" Gary said.

"Josie calls him Mike. And once he turned out to be kinda fun, I decided he seems

264

more like a Mike."

"I think I see," Gary said with a grin. "So tell me more about Josie, Lisa. How is she more than a nurse?"

"Can I tell him, Uncle Mike?"

"Tell him what?"

"About how my prayers have been answered."

Michael patted her on the shoulder. "Why don't you save that for later?"

Gary took off his sports coat, laid it across the back of a chair, then rubbed his hands together. "I'd love to hear all about it."

As Gary walked toward the couch, Michael could tell the exact moment he noticed the overloaded walls and the strange sketch. Gary made the slightest movement, almost like recoiling.

Michael had a feeling he was observing what he, himself, had looked like a week earlier. And it wasn't pretty. Lisa had been right about him being a snob.

"Josie's got a nice homey place here," Michael said. "Lisa has her own room. And the backyard is paradise. You should see the view."

"I'm sure," Gary said.

Michael checked his watch. "We're going to order some pizza in a while. Why don't you play a round of Monopoly with us, then hang around for dinner?"

"Sure. So tell me, Lisa, about your answered prayers."

Lisa smiled timidly at the floor. "I think God's going to make us a family."

"You and Michael?"

"No, silly. The —"

Josie's bedroom door opened. "I thought I heard voices." She stepped out and squinted at the bright light, her hair a chaotic mess. Her nose was still red from crying, and her eyes were as puffy as overstuffed pillows.

She was not going to be happy about meeting Gary like this. But what could he do? Send her back to her room?

"Hey, Josie," Lisa said. "Look who's here."

Chapter Fourteen

Josie blinked hard and tried to open her swollen eyes wide. Once she focused on the good-looking man standing in her living room, a replica of Mike, her face heated. She ran her hand through her wild mane. "Oh, hi. I'm Josie Miller." She offered her hand. A bumpy pattern from the bedspread was imprinted on it. Did her whole body and face look as if she'd been in a waffle iron? "You must be Gary. You're Mike with green eyes."

He shook her hand. "Yes, scary isn't it? Nice to meet you."

She wished she could say "nice to meet you." But right now she wanted to crawl back in her bed and hide until Gary left. Plus, he didn't look nearly as friendly as Mike. Of course, Mike hadn't been Mr. Personality in the beginning either. "I, uh, I'm a mess. I'll run and change."

"Michael told me you were up all night

with Lisa. Thanks for taking care of her." His words were gracious, but forced.

Thank you, Mike, for taking up for me. It definitely lifted her spirits to know he had.

"I was more than happy to watch Lisa last night. Although, she may not agree." Josie inched up Lisa's bandage to check her stitches. "Time to put on the ointment and change the dressing."

"Do you wanna see, Uncle Gary?"

"You bet. But only if Josie says it's okay."

"Sure. I'll bring the supplies out here."

While Josie was in the bathroom, she slapped the hairbrush at her tangles as if she were snuffing the life out of living creatures. For some reason, the jeans and T-shirt seemed too tight all of a sudden.

Why was she even worrying? Shouldn't she be good enough for Gary just the way she was? Why should he make her uncomfortable in her own home? Mike never had.

It only proved she was trying to impress Mike's brother.

This is wrong, wrong, wrong, Josie. This is why you left home. You never wanted to have to impress anyone ever again.

She tossed the hairbrush back in a drawer and ignored the call of the sink, begging her to wash her face and to press a cool cloth to the bags under her eyes.

If she and Mike were ever going to be anything together, then Gary would have to take her the way she was. She refused to be someone different around him.

She washed her hands, carried the ointment and bandage to the living room, then proceeded to doctor Lisa.

Once she'd removed the old dressing, she said, "Voila! Thirteen stitches for your viewing pleasure, Gary."

He gave Lisa a slow, sweet smile. Surprisingly, considering he looked just like Mike, it didn't do a thing for Josie. No three-point-two mile runs of the heart. But as he approached and made eye contact with Josie, his expression chilled. Or had she imagined it?

For Lisa's benefit, he examined the wound and whistled. "Wow. You must've been brave to let them shave your head and sew you up."

Lisa giggled, making her sound five years younger. "They almost had to tie me down."

Mike crossed his arms over his chest. "Once I sat on her long enough to prove that they had numbed the area, she calmed down. But that was after everyone in the E.R. had heard her screams."

"Oh, and what about you, Uncle Mike? Did ya tell 'em you about freaked when they put the needle through my skin?"

Josie pushed away her unease about Gary and had a good laugh at Mike. She couldn't imagine him ever freaking, being so out of control. "What did you do, Mike? Quietly, and ever so authoritatively, keel over?"

Mike jammed his hands on his hips, but his embarrassed smirk said he wasn't really mad. "I'll have you know that I merely broke out in a cold sweat and had to put my head between my knees. I would never be so undignified as to pass out — authoritatively or not."

Josie finished putting the bandage in place. "All done, Lisa."

"Are you going to eat with us, Uncle Gar?"

"I wouldn't miss it."

The way he glanced around the room, though, made him look anything but happy about it.

After another round of Monopoly, Michael watched Lisa eat three pieces of pizza. She'd had a hearty appetite all day, as if the scene at the hospital had been a turning point. Whatever the reason, he wouldn't take the blessing for granted.

Yet the scene around Josie's dinner table wasn't all he'd hoped. Gary had cooled toward Josie. And as a result, she'd become more reserved. It wasn't enough to affect Lisa, but he could feel the undercurrent. By the time they'd finished eating, the adult conversation had waned, and Lisa began to nod off.

"Off to bed, Lisa," Josie said. "You need sleep to finish healing."

"Uninterrupted sleep," she mumbled with her eyes half-closed.

"I promise I'll leave you alone tonight."

Lisa hugged Gary, then Josie. "Night."

For a moment, Michael was afraid she had forgotten him. But she came the long way around to hug him. And to kiss his cheek. "I love you Uncle Mike. Night."

"I love you, too, pumpkin." He managed to say the whole sentence before a lump fully wedged in his throat. He coughed to clear it out. "Sleep well."

After she left the kitchen, Michael caught Gary staring at him. "What?"

"I'm amazed at the transformation," Gary said. "You've done wonders."

"Josie's been the one keeping me straight."

"No, Mike's done all the work," she said. "I've only given suggestions."

"And she's called me a few choice names along the way. All well deserved, I might add."

Josie nodded. "Like *hopeless* . . . and —"

271

"I believe Gary gets the picture."

Gary looked back and forth between the two of them with narrowed eyes. "I believe I do," he said with a concerned frown.

"What's that supposed to mean?" Michael asked, his nerves on ultra-alert to the undertones of Gary's words.

"It means he probably sees the sparks flying between us," Josie said, hoping to irritate Gary. She was tired of the attitude he'd copped since he'd arrived and met her. "He's noticed the way you look at me with longing, with love, with total devotion. . . ." She smiled at Gary with the same condescending smile he'd been sporting.

Gary was a true competitor. He came right back with "Josie, you've been exactly what Michael and Lisa needed for this temporary family crisis. Thank you for all you've done." He slapped his knees and stood. "Now, if you'll give me a key to your house, Michael, I think I'll turn in. I need to leave early tomorrow. Unless you're going to go back to negotiate that contract?"

"What contract?" Josie asked. "You're leaving?" Forget the competition with Gary. She wanted answers.

Mike looked as if he'd been caught with his hand in the till. "Gary's run into a snag with Tom Mason."

"Why didn't you tell me? You've been talking like you were staying here a while longer no matter what."

"I hadn't decided what to do about Mason. I wanted to wait and see how Lisa was. Besides, Gary offered to stay while I'm gone."

Just what she wanted. The cautiously-cool-turned-antagonistic brother hanging around.

Gary stood and held out his hand. "The keys? I'll let you two talk."

Yeah, sure. Drop your bomb and head out. Well, she wouldn't stand for it. She hopped up to meet him eye to eye. "Gary, can I ask why you've taken such a dislike to me?"

He flushed, two big splotches of red streaking across his cheeks. "I'm just trying to protect Michael. I know you've done a great deal for Lisa. But my brother has his place back in Charleston. He needs to get back to work as soon as Lisa's ready."

"That's the plan. So what's bothering you?"

"I see more than that going on."

"No, there's not." But she knew better. There was definitely something brewing.

"And that would be between Josie and me if there were," Mike said.

"Whatever you say," Gary said as he

headed toward the kitchen door and rapid escape. "I'll leave you two to talk about Michael's trip to Charleston."

He was gone in a flash, the little chicken.

That left her alone with Mike and a syrupy thick silence. "Well. That was enlightening."

"I don't know what got into him."

"He thinks I'm not good enough for you."

"No, Gary's not like that. It's probably all about getting me home quickly, and he fears I'll want to stay."

"Because he figured out we may have feelings for each other."

"We do, don't we, Josie? Have feelings for each other?"

Her chest ached. Her throat tightened. She swallowed past the hurt of the evening. "Yes. Even though I don't want us to."

He placed his warm hands on her cheeks and rubbed his thumbs just below her eyes. She dared tears to fall where he would feel them.

"Could it be more? Love, even?" he asked.

She couldn't speak it. It would make it too real. Too scary. Especially since it was impossible. So she let her forehead fall against his chest and whispered, "I don't know."

He kissed the top of her head, then set

her away from him. "I'm going to go talk to him."

"What about going to Charleston?"

"I haven't decided. If I don't go, we'll lose the account. . . ." He waited as if wanting her to tell him to go.

She wouldn't make it that easy for him. It could devastate Lisa for him to go. She might interpret it as him backing out on her. As far as Josie knew, Mike hadn't even told Lisa that he wasn't sending her back to boarding school.

For once, Lisa needed Mike to choose her over everything else.

Josie did, too.

Michael let himself in the front door of his rental home and found his baby brother slouched on the couch. "Do you mind telling me what that scene was all about?"

"I'm just trying to keep you from getting hurt."

"I'm a big boy now and can handle it."

"Not where women are concerned."

"I think I'm falling in love with her." He'd stated it simply, when there was nothing at all simple about what he was feeling.

"You don't have to tell me. I can see it."

"I could really use your support, even though I still can't see my future with Josie.

At this point, I can't see her and Mother having lunch at the club."

"Don't make this mistake, Michael. Mother will eat Josie alive. She'll end up more hurt in the long run. And you might just end up out of a job and booted out of the family circle."

"Oh, I think I can hold my own. And I know Josie can. But I don't want her to have to."

Gary chuckled. "She handled me pretty well tonight."

"You deserved it. You were awful."

"I don't want you to start this war, big brother. Things at the bank are finally looking up for me — provided you'll hurry home for negotiations."

"If I go back to Charleston for you, will you promise to be nice to Josie?"

"I can guarantee I'll be nicer than Mother will be tomorrow. She'll want to protect her golden boy from a strange woman who could be after his money."

No way. Not now. "They're really coming?"

"Yes. They said they'd arrive around five."

What more could go wrong?

He sat in silence, waiting for the ceiling to fall in.

"If she could fit in better, then she would

276

stand a better chance of surviving a visit with Mother," Gary said. "Do you think —"

"Don't even think it, Gary. I wouldn't want to change a thing about her."

"Not change *her*. Just something little like having her dye her hair a color that's found in nature. Maybe buy a more conservative outfit."

Anger, and embarrassment for Josie, burned inside him. "You know nothing about it. The hair color was something nice she did for your niece."

Gary slowly unfolded himself from his lounging position on the couch. "I'm sorry. I'm shutting up and going to bed."

As Gary rattled around his luggage looking for a toothbrush, and Michael's temper settled, some of the ideas he'd had about the future began to take shape.

"What do you think of the idea of me turning over day-to-day bank operations to you?" Michael asked, wanting to test the waters. "I'd remain a stockholder, of course. I could work some from home so I'd be there for Lisa after school. Remaining on the board of directors of a couple of companies in the Southeast or doing consulting work would give me a nice income. And I wouldn't have to travel too much."

"You'd be in Charleston, though, right?"

"That's what I'm thinking."

Gary looked sorely tempted. "Do you really think I could handle the everyday operations?"

"What have you been doing for the last week?"

"Well, I may have lost a major client."

"That one's on me. It doesn't count. Over all, you did great."

"I have really enjoyed it. Dad seems surprised at the fact that I've managed as well as I have."

"I'm sorry he's never shown enough faith in you."

"And I'm sorry he's put so much pressure on you your whole life. I wouldn't have traded places."

"Until now." Michael smiled. "So, what do you think?"

"I think I'm not that easily bribed into changing my mind." He untucked his shirt and kicked off his shoes. "End it with Josie now, before you both get hurt. No woman is worth the damage this could cause your family and your career."

CHAPTER FIFTEEN

Early the next morning, Josie plopped herself down on a tall stool near the grill.

"So what brings you here on your day off?" Bud asked.

"Oh, nothin'."

"Uh-huh." He scraped bits of fried egg off the sizzling surface.

"What's that supposed to mean?"

"Feeling on edge, are we?"

She looked at the old man who'd been more of a father to her than her own father had been. And more of a mother than her own mother, for that matter. "I met Mike's brother last night."

"Meetin' the family so soon?" He set the spatula aside and wiped his hands on his apron.

"It's been nearly two weeks, thank you."

"It's been eleven days." He touched his finger to her forehead. "Have you lost your mind?"

"No. Only my heart."

"Seems to me you've lost both."

"The brother, Gary, hated me."

Bud's expression hardened. "Why, that no good —"

"He has good reason. He's worried about Mike leaving the bank, causing family strife."

"That makes it okay?" He walked around the counter and sat on the stool beside her. "I'm serious. I've been afraid that man would hurt you."

"I imagine Mike and I are afraid of the same thing."

"Of me taking out my shotgun?"

His overprotectiveness eased some of the tightness from her chest. She poked him in the arm. "No, silly. Of falling in love when our worlds don't fit together."

"But your world — the one you've been ignoring — does fit with his if you want it to."

"That's not the real me. I don't want the kind of life my parents had."

"Then tell Mr. Throckmorton goodbye and get back to your own peaceful life."

"Peaceful, *lonely* life."

He slid off the stool and headed for the grill. "Plenty of fellas out there."

"Just between you and me, there's no one

280

out there who makes me so happy."

"Happy like you are right now?"

She sighed loud enough for him to hear.

"Just be careful."

"You know, Bud, I've tried to be. But now I'm wondering if I should trust that God brought us together and has plans for us."

Bud stood and waved a hand at her. "You need to be realistic."

"I'm about as realistic as they come."

"Not where Throckmorton is concerned."

"My whole life I've been in self-protect mode. That's all good and fine if there's no one I'm interested in. But that's changed now. There's a good man whose company I enjoy, and who appears, wonder of all wonders, to care for me. He laughs at my jokes and likes me for me. The real me. And even though I can't imagine how we could possibly have a future, I'm tempted to risk giving him a chance."

"To risk getting hurt."

"Isn't every relationship a risk?"

He harrumphed.

"I like to think this is a God-thing, and want to have faith."

Bud sighed, then went back to his grill.

"If by some miracle he'll stay in Gatlinburg, we might have a chance to make this work. So I'm going out on a limb this time, Bud."

"If you fall off, you know you have a shoulder to cry on here at the diner."

Her tender heart bruised a little more. This man that she'd grown to love wouldn't be here for her forever. "Thank you. And —" She stood and hugged him. "I love you, you grouchy old man."

He patted her on the back. "I love you, too, you opinionated, hardheaded gal."

She laughed. "What would I do without you?"

With another dismissive wave of his hand, he slapped a sausage patty on the surface. "Oh, you can't get rid of someone as mean as me."

"So I'll have you here to bother me forever?"

"Yep. Looks like it. You tell that man he'll have to go through me if he thinks he's gonna marry you."

"We haven't come close to thinking about that."

"Oh, he will. I've seen it in that whipped-puppy look he gives you."

A little thrill caught in her belly, making it feel as if she were flying down Roller Coaster Road. Was Bud right? It wasn't like him to play around.

If only he were.

Josie sat on her bed studying the antique-looking portrait of Mike and her. She was struck by her expression of pure joy. She'd had a sense of completeness since she and Mike and Lisa had bonded. She'd found the family she had craved for so long. The family Bud had tried to give her the last couple of years.

The doorbell rang, and she rushed to the door and opened it.

"Hi." Mike stood on her front porch wearing a troubled expression. A far cry from the one in the photo.

"Hi to you. Where's Lisa?"

"I left her at my house eating breakfast."

"With Gary?"

"Yes."

She knew why he'd come, then. And why he didn't look happy. "So you're going to Charleston?"

"Yes. I should be back late tomorrow."

"How did she handle it?"

"Okay once she realized Gary would be staying."

So now Josie didn't have the excuse of worrying about Lisa. She should just go ahead and cry, *Don't leave me!* the way her mind was screaming. "Have a safe trip, then."

"So you're okay with my going?"

"Why wouldn't I be?" she snapped.

"All you have to do is say the word, and I'll stay."

"I wouldn't dream of stopping you," she said, way too waspishly. But, she wanted him to decide on his own.

Maybe she was being too scared. Then again, maybe he'd go home and forget about her. Forget what they'd had together.

Well, she would never know for sure if he didn't go.

"I know you and Gary had a rough start," he said. "But I talked to him last night. I think he'll behave."

She pressed her hand into his chest to stop him. "Do what you need to do. I'll deal with it."

"I'm afraid you may have to deal with my parents, too. They're driving up to check on Lisa and should be here late this afternoon."

"Well, that's just dandy. Bring 'em on. The whole Throckmorton clan."

"Josie . . ."

Resignation blotted out the fear. It was time to either move forward or give up. Yet she couldn't bear to think about the latter. "No. I'm serious. I may as well have my trial by fire. If your family and I survive the meeting without killing each other, then maybe when you come back, we can try this you-and-me thing and see where it leads."

He smiled his heartbreaking, knee-melting smile. "Thank you."

"Yeah, well . . ." She shooed him away.

He stepped closer, reached out, brushed a curl back from her temple. Would he finally kiss her?

She was ready this time. She nearly cried with the realization of how badly she wanted him to.

"Josie, I —"

She looked into his gorgeous blue eyes, hoping . . . waiting. . . .

"I've got to get on the road."

She blew out a deep breath, the one she'd been holding. Disappointment made her want to wail. Instead, she said, "Go. I'll hold down the fort."

"I promise I'll be back as soon as I possibly can. We'll talk then, about our future."

Her heart turned over, sending her world into slow motion. Before she could manage to utter a word, he smiled, then ran to his car. With a jaunty wave, he backed out and drove away.

Toward Charleston. Toward his home. Toward his real life.

Would he change back to the man who'd driven into town a couple of weeks ago?

She could only wait. And pray.

Gritting her teeth, Josie picked up the phone and called Gary. She was proud at how civilly she spoke. She even invited him and Lisa to come have dinner with her. He very graciously accepted. Then very smoothly suggested he take them out to eat since his parents would be joining them.

"You're smooth, Gary. Very smooth."

He chuckled, a lot like Mike. "How about we come over there at five o'clock when they're supposed to arrive?"

"Fine. I'll be here."

Once she hung up, she looked at herself in the full-length mirror on the back of her closet door. Pink hair. Grungy clothes. Her own mother wouldn't know her.

Did she have to look her worst for Mike's parents just to prove herself?

Lord, sometimes I don't know who I really am. I have this past that's so different from who I am now. Which is the real me? Since meeting Gary, I wonder.

Should I be ashamed of myself for even caring what he thinks?

If she humiliated herself in front of Mike's parents, it would only hurt him more.

286

Sure she might enjoy putting them in their place. She smiled just thinking about it. But if she had any chance of ever making a go of it with Mike, she couldn't just blatantly disrespect them.

Out of the blue, she recalled her dad pointing up the stairs, sending her to her room because she had embarrassed them if front of guests once again.

Well, she wouldn't embarrass anyone this time.

She would embrace her past. And she would start by phoning her parents.

Josie stared at the phone, willing it to dial itself. Willing it to make the phone call she was scared to make. She had apologized to her mother during the last call. But she hadn't really tried to talk, to work on forgiveness from both sides. Now she knew she had to if she was going to go on with her life and be a whole person.

She dialed the number, and this time her dad answered.

"Hi, Dad."

"Josephine? Is that you?"

"Yes, it's me. I hope Mom told you I called the other day."

"Well, yes, she did mention it."

"How was your golf game?"

"Same old, same old," he grumped in his gruff voice.

He was the same old, same old, too. Mr. Negative. "Dad, is Mom there? I'd like to talk to both of you."

"Hang on." He covered the mouthpiece. She heard a muffled, "Ruby Lee, pick up the phone. Josephine is on the line and wants to talk to us."

The line clicked. "Hi, baby. I'm so glad you called back when I could talk."

"Hi, Mom. Dad, are you still there?"

"Yes."

"I wanted to call and tell you both that I hope you will forgive me for all the trouble I caused as a teenager," she blurted before she lost the nerve. No talking about the weather for Josie Miller. "It's just that I always felt like I was under so much pressure. I didn't handle it well."

"I hope you can forgive us for our mistakes, too, Josephine."

So her mom did understand. "Yes, I forgive you. You know, no matter what I said or did, I always loved you both."

"I love you, too, honey," her mom said.

Silence from her dad.

"Ben?" her mom prompted.

"We love you, too, Josephine."

He couldn't say that he personally did,

but it was a start. At least Josie had opened up communication. "Well, that's what I wanted to say. I guess I'll let you go."

"Oh, don't go so quickly," her mom said. "Tell us what you've been up to."

"Well . . ." After so many years, she had no idea what to tell. "Like I mentioned the other day, I'm going to buy the diner where I work."

"You're going to buy that greasy spoon, huh?" her dad asked.

It *was* a greasy spoon, but she didn't appreciate him saying so. It felt like a slight to Bud. "The owner, who's been very good to me, is retiring due to a back injury. I'm taking it over, buying it when I get the down payment saved."

"Do you need some money?" her dad asked. To him, everything came down to dollar signs.

"No. I've got a nice little nest egg saved."

"Well . . ." He cleared his throat. "If you need anything, you know the number."

"Do you have a man in your life?" her mom tossed out there, having no idea that it was the sixty-million-dollar question.

"A man?" her dad asked in the same tone of voice he'd used to disparage his golf game. "Goodness, Ruby Lee. Don't interrogate the girl, or she won't call back."

Josie's stomach fluttered at his comment. Could he really be saying he wanted her to keep calling? "It's okay. I've actually recently met someone."

"Oh, Josephine, I'm so happy for you," her mom said.

"He's a banker, very responsible, kind. And he's guardian for his niece, whose mother died."

"Oh, my. You'd be an instant mother," her mother said.

A smile stole across Josie's face as she thought of her potential family. "This is all new and up in the air right now. It might not get to that point."

"A banker, huh? Tellers don't make much. Could he support you?" her dad asked.

Josie fought the whoop of laughter that just about slipped out. Someday when they met Mike, she'd let Mike straighten them out. "He makes plenty, Dad."

"I hope you'll let us know if it gets serious," her mom said.

"I will." She just hoped she had good news to tell them eventually. "Well, I should get going. I need to make a hair appointment. I'm supposed to meet his parents this evening." She didn't include the fact that he'd gone out of town on business leaving her to the wolves.

"You'll have to call and let us know how it goes. In the meantime, we'll figure out when we can come up there to see you, won't we Ben?"

"Uh, yeah. Sure."

Josie could see it now — her mom heading to Gatlinburg, dragging her dad behind.

It was just as well he was so resistant. She didn't need to deal with a reunion any time soon. Mike's parents would be enough on anyone's plate.

CHAPTER SIXTEEN

Michael got as far as the interstate before Lisa called.

Even though she had said she didn't mind him leaving, he still couldn't shake the memory of the expression on her face — a touch of anger, a touch of fear. He imagined that she might fear he wouldn't come back. Or that he would change his mind and let her down once again.

He could only guess what went on in that teenaged female brain.

"Hey, it's me," she said.

"What's up?"

"How far are you?"

"Just got on the highway."

"I see . . ." Silence.

"What's Uncle Gary doing?"

"Setting up the Monopoly board. We borrowed Josie's."

Oh, good. He's trying to keep her occupied.
"Sounds fun."

She sighed. "I guess." More silence.

"Are you okay?"

"Yeah, I guess. I just —"

"What, pumpkin?"

"Are you really coming back?"

"Yes. I promise."

"You're sure? I mean, you won't go all Dr. Jekyll and Mr. Hyde on me, will you?"

"Excuse me?"

"You know, Dr. Michael, Mr. Mike? Go back to your old self?"

She sounded so pitiful, guilt struck full force. "No, no reversals back to the old Michael for me. You and Josie have cured me."

"You promise?"

"Yes."

"You still love me?"

"Of course."

"And you won't forget about me, even if Mr. Mason's a pain or when you see all the mail piled up?"

"Never."

"Okay." She heaved a sigh. "Call me when you get there."

As they said their goodbyes, he remembered two times in the past year that he had promised her he'd go visit her on the weekend but had failed to keep his promise. Of course he hadn't stood her up. No, he was too organized for that. He'd had his secretary call to cancel.

It was no wonder she was having doubts. He would too if he were in her shoes.

And now was the time when she needed him most. When they were finally forming a relationship.

When she was learning to trust that he'd be there for her from here on out.

What had he been thinking? How could he have left Lisa for Tom Mason — for a business deal?

He dialed her back, and she answered before the end of the first ring.

"Hey, pumpkin. You and Gary set that Monopoly board for three. I'm turning around right now."

She whooped in his ear as he zoomed off the next exit and headed in the other direction. He left a voice mail for Mason, telling the truth about his niece, and how he couldn't leave her. He apologized and told him Gary would be taking over for him — Mason would have to work with Gary.

Once he'd finished that business, it seemed to take forever before he finally arrived at his rental house.

When he walked in the front door, Gary shook his head and frowned. "So this is it."

"I couldn't leave Lisa, even if just for a day or two."

"Couldn't leave Josie, either?"

"This time it was about our niece."

"And when it's about Josie? I don't see it happening."

"Josie and I have a lot to figure out. But I'm hoping to make a way for her to eventually come to Charleston."

"I hope you know what you're getting into." Gary stuffed his belongings into his designer bag. "You have a date with Josie, Lisa and our parents today. Meet at Josie's at five o'clock. Dinner out later."

"Thanks, Gar. I left Mason a message. Told him you're in charge. We'll see what he decides."

"This is a mistake."

"I couldn't walk away and leave Lisa."

"Dad's not going to be happy."

"We all — Mother and Dad included — are going to have to make adjustments."

"Adjustments for Lisa are one thing. Adjustments for Josie are entirely different."

"It'll all work out."

Gary shook Michael's hand — no hug this time. "Let's hope."

"Let's hope . . . and pray," Michael said to himself as Gary drove away.

Michael sat across from Lisa at the card table he'd set up in his dining room. She tossed the dice in her hands. "Is Josie coming over to play Monopoly with us?"

"Can't. She has a hair appointment."

"Oh! Maybe she's gonna do it."

"Do what?"

"Get her hair dyed green."

"What?"

"Way back when I talked about dreading seeing Grandmother and Grandfather again because of my hair, she said she ought to color hers in solidarity with me."

He stood and paced the wooden floor of the tiny room. "You don't think she would really do that, would she?" He could envision his mother fainting dead away.

Lisa laughed — more like a whoop. "If she does, she's my hero."

Of course, Josie would. It was *exactly* what she would do.

And he would love her for it. But she couldn't have picked a worse time.

"I can't wait for Grandmother and Grandfather to get here." Lisa couldn't stop laughing as she rolled the dice and moved her game piece. "This is going to be so cool."

Michael's parents pulled in the driveway at precisely five o'clock. Normally that would have impressed him. Today, it frustrated him.

Especially with Josie's car still gone and Lisa hiding out at Josie's house.

Michael met his parents at his front door.

"Darling, it's so good to see you." His mother gave him a cheek-to-cheek air kiss to save her lipstick.

"Son." His dad offered a handshake. "Cute little place you've got here."

"It's rather bare, but it's worked fine for what I need."

"Where's Lisa?" his mother asked.

"She's waiting over at Josie's house."

"Why can't she just come on home with you? She's getting behind in her classes." His mother clutched her purse to her as if she might be robbed.

"Come on. Let's go across the street, and you can see Lisa, then meet Josie when she gets home."

His dad held out his arm for his wife. "Gary tells me you care for this Josie."

He stifled his irritation with Gary. "Yes, sir. I know you'll like her."

His mother picked her way carefully across the street, making sure not to trip on bits of grass that were trying to peek through cracks in the pavement. "Does Josie live there? In that pinkish house?"

"Yes, she does. She's been here a couple of years. Just to warn you, it's not decorated like yours, but it's comfortable, and Lisa loves it here. Josie has taken good care of your granddaughter. You should be thankful."

His mother raised her perfectly drawn eyebrows at his speech. "Of course we are, dear."

He climbed Josie's front steps and knocked. But his parents remained on the walk below, his mother's arm hooked through his dad's as if they were being presented at the prom.

No one answered. Great. Lisa really was going to stay concealed until Josie arrived. He smiled at his parents, then took out his key and opened the door. "Come on in. Lisa probably couldn't hear us knock."

His parents followed him in, his dad frowning at the key as if the fact Michael had one meant something inappropriate.

Michael had to give them credit. They were very discreet as they checked out Josie's interior.

"Have a seat," he said. "I'll find her." He hollered toward the bedrooms, "Lisa, we're here."

Lisa squealed. "I'll be out in a minute."

"Should we go back to my house?" he called, wishing they could avoid this whole scene.

"No. Josie called to say she's on her way."

He sighed in relief as he sat in the chair. At least Josie hadn't backed out on them. Of course, if she showed up with green hair, he might wish she had.

"I know what a handful Lisa's been. Josie must be a patient woman," his dad said.

"Josie's been great, Dad. She's been a mediator for us. Without her help, I have a feeling Lisa would have run away again."

"Then that's definitely a mark in her favor," his mother said.

She would need all the marks she could get.

Without warning, Lisa came bounding into the room, green hair spiked around the bandage. "Here I am!"

Why hadn't she waited for Josie?

"Oh, Lisa, what have you done to your beautiful hair?" his mother said as she stood to hug and kiss her. "Oh, never mind. I've missed you so. Are you feeling okay?"

"I've missed both of you. And, yes, I'm fine." She hugged her grandfather.

"Of all colors. Why green?" his mom said, unable to let the topic drop.

"Oh, I'm sure you'd be surprised how many other people color theirs green." She turned to look at Michael, then winked.

She was enjoying this entirely too much.

"Well, maybe I can take you to my colorist as soon as we get home."

"Thanks, Grandmother, but I'm happy with it right now. How about some hors d'oeuvres, everybody? I made some while Josie was out."

Impressed, he said, "That would be great. Thanks, Lisa."

She practically skipped to the kitchen, humming along the way.

"I'm impressed, Michael," his dad said. "She's like a new child."

"Yes. And we'll want to thank Josie," his mother said. "Is there something we can get for her to show our appreciation?"

He almost laughed. "Oh, no. Please don't. I've tried, and she won't hear of it."

Lisa came back in the room carrying a tray with several cheeses and rolled up ham. "Here you go."

A car door slammed out front.

"Oh, there she is!" Lisa ran her hands through her hair, then grinned at him.

A moment later, the front door opened. There stood a complete strang—

He nearly swallowed his tongue. "Josie?"

She walked straight toward his parents, smiling and held out her hand to shake with his father, then his mother. "Hi, I'm Josie Miller."

Michael remembered his manners and introduced them.

He could hardly pull his attention from Josie. But he knew he had to check on Lisa.

Lisa tried to smile, but she couldn't seem to quit staring at Josie. And glaring. "Hi, Josie. Wow. You look different."

In an awkward gesture, Josie glanced at his parents, then spun around. "Whadaya think? New hairdo."

"I'll say," Lisa said. And she wasn't happy.

Michael wasn't so sure he was happy, either.

He took her by the shoulders and looked her square in the eye. Really hard. Just to make sure it was her.

"Mike, say something."

He blinked. "Wow." Standing before him was a beautiful woman with golden-brown hair, cut in a sleek shoulder-length style that had miraculously smoothed the curl out. She wore an expensive-looking, teal-colored linen suit and stockings. High-heeled shoes, too. No orthopedic, squeaky-soled clunkers here.

"Mike? You call him Mike?" his dad asked.

"Yes. Don't you think it fits his new image better?"

His dad smiled. "New image?"

"Tell them, Lisa," Josie said.

"We've been working on him to loosen up," Lisa said to her grandparents. "And Uncle Mike's gotten pretty cool." She sent Josie an angry glare. "But it looks like someone else has been finding a new image, too. One that Grandmother would love."

"Pardon me?" his mother said.

Lisa examined her fingernails. "I told her to dress up to impress you. That's all."

Josie walked toward Lisa. Nothing jingled. Not a ring or bracelet anywhere. She wore only a classy string of pearls around her neck and pearl studs in her ears. They looked almost real.

Lisa was right. His mother would approve of this version of Josie.

"Lisa, honey, are you okay?" Josie asked.

"I hope you didn't spend all your savings."

Josie smiled, but barely. She looked worried. "No. The dress and stuff, it's all . . . used."

"So that's why you're late? You've been hitting the flea markets this morning?"

"It's actually mine. From a long time ago."

"Yeah, well, I've got to go feed the cat."

Lisa hustled toward the kitchen and out the back door, letting the screen door slam.

Sure enough, his parents would love this Josie. She had it all. All except for the pedigree.

But she'd let Lisa down. It made him hurt to think of how excited Lisa had been that Josie was at an appointment to get her hair dyed green.

"Lisa sure doesn't seem very happy all of a sudden," his mother said.

"I'm afraid that's my fault." Josie sat in the chair across from them. "I've surprised her with a new hair color and look. Not a good surprise, obviously."

"Well, you look lovely, dear. Maybe you can help me convince Lisa to have her hair changed back to her normal color once we get home."

"I think she's happy like she is."

"Well, I must say she's improved greatly," his mother said, awe and maybe a little respect in her voice. "You two have done wonders getting her out of her angry, silent phase."

"I owe it all to Josie," Michael said. "I didn't handle Lisa well when I first got here."

Josie laughed. "All he wanted to do was get back to the bank and to some important dinner meeting. But he seems to have found his calling. To care for Lisa."

Oh, boy. Just what he needed. For Josie to bring up the bank before he could ease his parents into the subject.

Michael's dad nodded his head. "I see. So you've found your calling, son? And it doesn't involve getting back to work?"

"Actually, sir, I'm trying to make Lisa a priority, and I'm weighing my options as to how I can work it out."

"Your mother's right, Michael. It's time to come home."

His mother got up and moved toward the kitchen where Lisa had gone. "Why don't I go talk to her? I'll help her pack her things, and we'll leave tomorrow."

"Lisa isn't going anywhere." Michael ushered his mother back to her seat. "She's happy here, and until we feel she's ready to go back to Charleston, I'm staying, too."

"What about the bank?" his dad asked.

"We need to talk about that."

"Then let's talk."

"Here's what I've been thinking." Michael paced across the floor toward the front door, then back. "I'm thinking of naming Gary COO."

His mother gasped. "You what?"

"He's perfect for it. And he loves it."

"But we groomed you for that position. You've done an excellent job. Gary hasn't had time to prove himself yet."

"Gary will do an excellent job, too," Michael said.

"What would you do, then?" his father asked.

"A lot of the same things I do now, only Gary would be in charge. I would keep my stock and stay on the board of directors. I would have to cut back to serving on only one or two corporate boards. And I can do a lot of work at home by computer in the afternoons."

"I don't want you working halfheartedly," his dad said. "You need to decide whether you're onboard or not."

Was his dad giving him an ultimatum?

"Of course I'm onboard, sir. I'm just assigning some of my duties to Gary. It's time he was promoted anyway."

"You can't work in a family-owned business by computer. Personal service has been our hallmark since we opened our doors. How will Heyward Gasque feel if he calls to talk to you and gets some automated menu telling him to contact you by voice mail or e-mail?"

"I don't envision that happening," he said. "I'll be there during school hours."

"And what about when old Mrs. LaBorde comes in to withdraw her weekly allowance and has to deal with a teller? She'll be so confused she'll end up in the hospital again."

"That's what Gary will handle so I can get away any time I need to."

"Mrs. LaBorde has asked for you for nearly ten years."

"I haven't worked out all the details yet."

His mother looked encouraged. "He would be more available when Lisa has school functions for him to attend. And maybe knowing her uncle was more available would encourage her to come home."

"I'm hoping so, Mother. And I guess I should tell you I want Lisa to live at home with me."

"She's seems to be doing well. That should be fine," his dad said.

"That's wonderful, dear. I'm sure she'll come home when you tell her that."

Josie wasn't so sure she liked the way the discussion was going. The plan didn't seem to include her. She raised her hand as if in school. "But Mike —"

"Josie, I'm thinking about it, okay? It could work. We could live in my house with Lisa. She could go to her school as a day participant. Or even to public school."

"We? As in you and Lisa — and me?"

He looked embarrassed to have said the all-inclusive word. "Well, sure. Maybe. I've been considering it."

"Are you talking marriage?" his mother asked, and he thought she might pop the vein in her neck.

"No, Mother. We're just —"

"But you've never talked about me moving to Charleston. How can you toss out that idea right now? What about the diner?"

"The diner?" his mother asked.

"I'm going to buy the diner where I work."

"And where might that be?"

"Near here. Bud's Diner. I'm a waitress there."

Mike's mother's eyebrows rose again. "But Michael and Lisa can't possibly remain here permanently."

The doorbell rang, throwing an unnatural silence over everyone.

Saved by the bell. The stupid thought rang over and over in her mind as she went to the front door and opened it.

"Oh, Josie, honey. I can't believe it's really you." She reached for Josie.

Josie leaped back, startled.

A man — her father — stood wide-eyed, staring. "Josephine, you look exactly the same."

This can't be happening right now.

"Oh my goodness, come here. Let us hug you," Josie's mother said.

Josie's face scorched with embarrassment at the awkward public reunion.

This wasn't at all what she'd envisioned when she'd imagined seeing her parents again for the first time in years. What rotten timing. She wanted to cry in her frustration, but hugged them instead.

It was almost like hugging strangers. They had aged so much. They even felt different, a little rounder, softer. And her dad seemed smaller. Not as threatening as she remembered.

Josie stood aside and motioned them in. "Mom and Dad, come in. I'd like you to meet my, uh, good friend. And his parents."

CHAPTER SEVENTEEN

Michael's heart dropped to his feet. Josie's parents? *Oh, Lord, why now? This can't be happening.*

The late-afternoon sun streaming in the open door created a glare, so Michael couldn't see them. He went to welcome them, dreading the scene. Here was the abusive, beer-swilling, table-belching father. And the poor, overworked mother.

"Mom, Dad, this is Mike."

He shaded his eyes as Josie closed the door. When at last he could see them, he stopped dead in his tracks. These weren't the characters of the police drama he'd pictured. "These are your parents?"

"Yes. Ben and Ruby Lee Miller."

"Ben Miller?" Michael's dad asked from across the too-small room. "Benjamin Thomas Miller of Miller Enterprises?"

Ben looked across the room. "Is that you, Junior?"

Michael was sure the shock on his own face mirrored the look of disbelief on Josie's. "Your dad is Ben Miller?" he said to Josie.

"Yes. Do you know him?"

"I know *of* him. Through Dad."

"My goodness, it's been years," said Michael's mother.

The women hugged and the men shook hands.

Michael and Lisa — who had slipped in at some point — stood to the side. Josie's mom hugged her some more. Michael suspected he saw a few tears in Ruby Lee's eyes, eyes that looked just like Josie's except for the tired-looking wrinkles around them.

He still couldn't believe the scene before him. *His* Josie was one of *those* Millers?

"Well, Josephine, you've certainly come up in the world," her dad said. "Most people would consider snagging a Throckmorton a coup." He looked proud enough to crow.

Michael's dad smiled, but still appeared to be in shock. "I'd say both our kids have made a surprising match. Imagine, after all these years . . ."

"Why didn't you tell us who Josie was, dear?" his mother asked him.

He stared at Josie as he answered. "Because she never bothered to tell me."

"Or me, either," Lisa said in a pitiful voice

from the doorway into the kitchen.

"Lisa, these are my parents. Mom, Dad, this is Mike's niece, the girl I was telling you about. She's been staying with me."

"You have got to be the biggest liar I know." Huge tears rolled down Lisa's face. "You went and got your hair done up, dressed up all nice — Miss pearls in the ears — all the time acting like a poor waitress. And you're really one of them. A rich snob, no better than all the girls at my school."

"It's not like that."

"How could you lie to me? You, of all people?"

"I never lied. This isn't the real me. It's just . . ."

What was it besides a huge mistake? Why hadn't she thought?

Lisa laughed, but it caught in her throat in the middle of a sob. "I told Uncle Mike you were out dying your hair green in solidarity with me." She huffed in a quivery breath. "How stupid did that make me look, huh?"

"Oh, Lisa, I'm sorry. I was just trying to make everything easier for Mike. I should have thought of you, too."

"I don't want to hear it. I wouldn't believe a word you said anyway." She turned to

Mike. "I'm going to go pack." Then she ran to her room and slammed the door.

"Josie, dear, I'm sorry if we've come at a bad time." Her mom looked distressed. "Maybe we should go."

"No. Stay. We'll just . . ." She waved her hand around the room in general, totally at a loss.

"Josie, can I speak to you outside, please?"

It was Mike. And he wasn't happy. Of course he wasn't. How else could he feel when she had devastated his niece with her makeover and secret past? "Sure. Out on the deck. The rest of you, well, make yourselves at home."

How lame was that? She'd made a total disaster of the day and she was trying to play hostess.

As she walked through the kitchen and out the back door, she prayed that God would comfort Lisa.

Lord, why did I try to be someone I'm not, just to impress Mike's parents? It's exactly what I didn't want to do. And I fooled myself into believing it was best for everyone. But I was just trying to take the easy path.

I've been such a fool.

Michael followed Josie outside and leaned over the deck railing. "Would you care to inform me why you never told me about your family?"

"I did tell you about them. I just never named them."

"You led me to believe they were some kind of country bumpkins, and that your father was abusive."

"I led you?" She scowled at him. "You know good and well you took one look at me and made up your mind that they were country bumpkins."

"But you said your dad was a tyrant."

"He was. Probably still is. That's not a trait exclusive to the poor."

"You've acted like you don't have a dime to your name."

"I don't. Just what I've earned and saved."

He paced across the wooden deck. "I don't get it. You could have called and asked for the money to buy the diner. Yet you've been scraping and saving." He pointed to her hair. "You wouldn't even use enough of your savings to get your pink hair fixed."

He plunked into a chair, then stood back up. "I feel like a fool. You had to know what I was thinking, yet you let me go on thinking all the wrong things about you."

"Speaking of feeling like a fool . . . Apparently, I've been delusional in thinking you and Lisa and I had some wild chance at forming a family — here in Gatlinburg."

"I can work out a schedule that fits Lisa's needs, but I would have to be there, in Charleston, for the bank."

"But we need you. *I* need you." It was the scariest admission she'd ever made. But she had to do it. She refused to act as if she didn't have serious feelings for him.

No more holding back. No more misunderstandings.

Her heart pounded as he seemed to consider what she'd said.

Michael was surprised at her honesty. Yet not really. She had always spoken her mind. He took hold of her hand. "Then come with me. We can buy you a diner there."

She recoiled as if he'd slapped her. "You just don't get it, do you? Bud is counting on me. He's sent away other buyers and has waited for me."

"Then invite him to move with you. Hey, we can even open you a jewelry boutique."

"The diner belonged to his dad, Mike. I can't do that to him." She stood and began to pace. "I don't get why you're pushing on this. You said you don't enjoy your work at the bank."

"I'm excited about this new plan to put Gary in charge."

"But do you feel called to be there?"

"I still don't have a real sense of direction.

But they're my family, Josie. And the bank is my life. I can't totally walk away."

"And neither can I."

Michael had feared it might come down to this. An impasse. Because of duty. But he had been so hopeful she was The One that he'd thought they could work out the logistics.

He couldn't imagine leaving her here in her little diner. It hurt too bad to consider it.

"So, there's no 'us,' huh?" she asked.

"I want there to be."

"Yeah, me, too. I guess sometimes, instead of what we want at the moment, we have to choose our dreams and the path our life is on already."

Josie wanted to cry, and to stomp her foot, but she couldn't manage either one. She couldn't force him to love her enough to give up his home and family. And why would he want to when she wasn't willing to give up her own dreams and aspirations?

"I guess we'll have to talk to Lisa." She absolutely did *not* want to do that, especially when everything inside her ached, felt raw.

She and Michael were going to break Lisa's heart.

"I'll find her and talk to her," he said. "I'm

afraid she's too angry with you right now."

"At least you're going to let Lisa live with you. I hope you'll let her go to public school."

"I will if you think it's best."

"For her, yes. At least I'll have the consolation of knowing I've accomplished what I set out to do."

"Thank you, Josie." He held his hand out to shake. The gesture cut her to the quick.

She shook his hand, then stifled a sob. She turned and walked back into the kitchen. She gathered herself — a feat that would impress her mother — and walked, smiling, into the living room. "Sorry to be gone so long. Are you enjoying your reunion?" she asked the parents.

"Oh, we are, dear. It's been a wonderful day," her mom said. "We've just been telling them how today has been a reunion with you, as well."

Great. Another reason for Mrs. Throckmorton to hate her. Of course, that wouldn't matter anymore.

"We're so tickled that you and Michael have feelings for each other," her never-to-be mother-in-law said.

"Yessiree, Josephine, you've made your old dad proud." He nearly beamed.

Of course, the one time she'd made her

dad proud had only lasted about ten minutes.

It was time to tell them that *feelings* weren't enough.

Michael stared out into Josie's backyard. He would miss the green of her trees, the cool crisp air, the mountains nearby.

No time to be sentimental. He had a job to do. Unpleasant, but necessary, nonetheless.

He walked toward the kitchen, but found Lisa already standing there just inside the screen door. "Oh. I was coming to find you."

She opened the door and stepped outside. "I figured you would soon. I heard."

"What do you mean, you heard?"

"I was in my room and heard Josie telling the parents that the two of you won't be a couple. That your lives are too set for either of you to move." She couldn't look him in the eye. "I'm sorry. I know you really liked her."

He let his head drop and sighed. Nothing about the day had gone right. "Yeah. But sometimes feelings aren't enough. Love, even, isn't enough." He put his arm around her shoulders. "Come on, let's talk about how this affects you."

They sat side by side on the steps leading

from the deck to the yard. The supposed stray cat inched toward them and began to wind its way around Lisa's legs, purring almost as loudly as a car engine rattling down the street out front.

After waiting while the car engine faded away, he said, "I'm sorry you had to hear the news that way."

"Yeah, well, life stinks sometimes. Today is one of those days."

His thoughts exactly. "I know."

"I guess I'm ready to go back to school. I'll be good this time, I promise."

He couldn't blame Lisa's insecurity on Josie. He was the one who had let his niece down over and over. Well, no more. "I want to ask you a favor."

She shrugged. "Okay."

It was amazing to him how simply she agreed. No strings attached. No maybes. Just "okay," as if he hadn't recently dashed the dreams and prayers she'd shared.

"It's time for me to go back to Charleston," he said. "I'd be honored if you'd come live with me."

She sat up straighter. "Live with you — at your house?"

"Yes. You can fix up your very own room."

"For good? Not just temporarily?"

"For good. Like a real family." He

smoothed his hand over her spiky hair. "You can go to public school if you'd prefer. I promise you can be yourself."

She smiled, tears in her eyes. "Thank you, Uncle Mike."

CHAPTER EIGHTEEN

Josie dragged through the diner, trying to perk up so Bud would quit worrying. But it was hard to smile and expend energy she didn't feel.

She missed Mike. And she missed Lisa. Desperately.

She even missed the allergen-filled cat since Lisa had taken it with her.

"Josie," Bud yelled.

She jerked, shocked at his tone. "What?"

"I've been calling your name. Order's up."

"Oh, sorry."

"Get over here once you deliver that burger. We need to talk."

So far, Bud had resisted saying *I told you so*. But she saw it in every look he gave her.

Well, that wasn't really true. Most of the looks he gave her held pity, which grated. She'd rather he boasted about being right.

She'd had two whole weeks to get over Lisa and Mike. She'd even had another teenager with her for five of those days. But now the girl had gone home — a good thing. Still, it left the house empty. Quiet. Devoid of the sense of family she'd grown used to while Lisa had been there.

How could she have let the desire to please his parents ruin everything?

Of course, that wasn't the whole picture. She and Mike couldn't have made it no matter what her hair or wardrobe looked like. No matter who her parents were.

Still, two weeks later, disappointment made her bones denser, heavier, made it harder to move through the days at the diner. She had thought Mike was tougher. She'd thought he might love her enough to blow convention to the wind. Instead, they'd each declared where their loyalties lay.

But I trusted him. I went out on that limb.

After delivering the burger, then refilling a glass of iced tea, she sat across from Bud, who waited in a booth. He gave her a sad smile.

"Don't look at me like that. I'm not going to break."

"If you say so."

"I'm just down. I'll get over it."

"When? Once you work yourself to death here at the diner?"

"It's a balm. And a way to forget."

"What are you trying to forget?"

"How I messed everything up. I let that child down. I went against everything I stand for right when she needed me the most."

"What about Throckmorton?"

"He did what he had to do. But it feels like he let me down."

"So, do you think he's beating himself up right about now?"

"No, and he shouldn't be. As far as letting Lisa down, I'm the one who messed up."

"Just trying to make him happy. So go easy on yourself."

"Yeah, yeah, we all make mistakes. I know. You've said it every day about a thousand times."

"Well, you either forgive yourself and move on, or you do something about it."

"Like what?"

"Apologize."

"I did that. She didn't even want to talk to me."

"She was hurt. I'm sure time has helped."

"Maybe later. It's too soon."

"Are you afraid of making contact with the uncle?"

Just thinking of it sent her pulse racing. She couldn't imagine having to face him, or talk to him. Surely she would cry or do something to embarrass herself.

She missed Mike so bad. Missed his voice, his laugh, his particular ways.

But he had his life, and she had hers. And the two couldn't possibly mix.

"At least I have my mom and dad again."

"Yeah, they'll be around to keep you company in your old age."

"Oh, hush. I've got a life to live. And even if I'm not sparkling happy at the moment, I have you, my parents, my church, my calling and this diner to fill my life. The happy part will come again later."

"Whatever you say, Josie, whatever you say." He grunted as he stood and headed back to the grill, rubbing his back just below the tie of his apron.

Why did he try to make her feel worse right when she thought she was making some headway?

Well, maybe not headway, exactly. But at least she was getting out of bed in the morning and going through the motions.

The problem was no matter what relationship she had with her parents or Bud, it couldn't replace what she'd lost when Mike had given up on their love.

Michael cut his dad off mid-sentence.

Granted, the man was complaining, and Michael was looking for an escape route already. But it was five minutes past his absolute latest time to leave the bank. He had to leave now or Lisa would arrive home before him. And he still didn't like the idea of her going into an empty house.

"Sorry, Dad. Gotta run. We'll finish this tomorrow." He grabbed his jacket and stood in one swift motion as his dad sputtered in aggravation and maybe a little shock.

"Excuse me?"

"Gotta meet Lisa."

His dad grunted, but let Michael pass and hurry out of the bank. He waved at the tellers as he left. They knew to go to Gary, the new chief operating officer, if they needed anything.

Michael hurried through afternoon traffic and reached the driveway at the same moment as Lisa from the opposite direction. She tooted her horn at him. He waved out the window.

Once they parked and got out, he carried her backpack inside for her, the weight of it staggering. "How do you carry this thing all the time?"

"I've got two tests tomorrow. Two big textbooks."

"Is that why the glum expression?"

She sighed as if she had more than the weight of the backpack to endure. "No."

"School go okay?"

"Sure. Everyone's great."

She had been wearing her chain belts and black shirts to the public school but had continued to wear the jeans they'd bought together. He was hoping she would make the right kind of friends. Of course, she had fussed at him for that attitude already. He had to be careful what he said.

"So you're making friends?"

"Yeah. I've met one really nice girl whose family knows our family, if that's any consolation."

"Then why the sigh?"

"I miss Josie."

"Yeah, me too, pumpkin." He ruffled her hair. "Let's get you something to eat before you study."

They'd settled into a nice routine since moving her home and getting her enrolled in school. His life was more complete than he'd ever imagined.

Yet it wasn't complete. And he was beginning to believe it never would be.

He opened the fridge and pulled out a block of cheese. "How about cheese and crackers?"

"And some grapes? Just like Josie always

gave me."

He chuckled. "Are you trying to get me to talk about her?"

"Do you want to?"

Sure, he'd love to talk about her. But it only made it more painful not to see her. He'd sure thought about her enough and had begun to wonder if God was trying to tell him something. "I wouldn't mind."

"Why can't we go see her, Uncle Mike? To try to make up."

"What about how hurt you were that she didn't dye her hair green?"

"Oh, I've gotten over that. When I really thought about it, I realized she didn't do it to make herself look good. She did it for you. Because that's just how she is."

Yeah, that's just how she is. "I guess you're right."

"So can we go see her?"

"We could. But it won't change anything. She has Bud, the diner, her runaway ministry. She's as tied to Gatlinburg as we are to Charleston."

"How tied are we?"

He sliced two perfect pieces of cheddar, then focused on opening the pack of crackers. "Aren't you happy here?"

"Of course I am."

"Then why are you asking?"

She hung her head. "I like being tied here in Charleston. Or I guess it's really that I like being tied to you, not the place. But it's like you and I are two ends of a shoelace, nicely tied, but we've lost the shoe we were tied to." She laughed. "I tried all day to think of a way to describe it, but that was stupid. So forget it."

She's right. The realization hit him like a jab to the solar plexus, stealing his breath.

Everything was fine on the surface. He and Lisa had a great setup. She loved her new school. She had friends. Gary was doing excellent work at the bank, so Michael was free to leave early.

But in the weeks they'd been gone and he'd prayed for confirmation that his calling was at the bank, he hadn't had any sense of being on the right track. He'd enjoyed the more relaxed schedule at work. But still, no feeling at peace, no sense that he was where God wanted him to be.

He and Lisa had a satisfying routine. But the heart of everything was gone.

We've lost our heart. Our shoe.

He laughed at the silliness of Lisa's description.

"What's funny?"

"Josie *is* our shoe. She's the glue that kept us together."

Lisa grinned. "She's our duct tape."

"Our anchor," he said and wrapped an arm around Lisa's shoulders, giving a squeeze.

"The foundation of our house." She giggled and reached for a grape.

"Our FDIC?"

"Bad one, Uncle Mike. Won't work."

He leaned against the counter and watched Lisa eat her snack.

Lord, am I supposed to be in Gatlinburg, with Josie?

"So what are we going to do?" Lisa asked, then proceeded to lick sticky juice off her fingers.

Simply talking about Josie brought joy to their lives. *This is what you want, isn't it, Lord?*

The peace that had been missing seemed to flow over him all at once. Tension that had been a constant companion eased away from his neck, his shoulders.

Confirmation. Finally.

Michael knew it was up to him to make the first move in Josie's direction.

Lord, I want to make the right decisions. I've been no good at this love business, though. Please help me figure out how best to love Josie and Lisa. I can't do it without You.

He grabbed his cell phone and looked up a phone number in the address book. He had some calls to make.

"Lisa, whadaya say we plan a trip to Gatlinburg?"

"For real?"

"An extended trip. I suppose one public school is as good as another, isn't it?"

Her mouth fell open. "Are you saying what I think you're saying?"

"I imagine so."

"How?"

"I have no idea. We'll have to let God work out the details."

She threw herself into his arms the way she had in Gatlinburg. "You're the best!"

Setting her aside, he said, "Hang on a minute. We have no idea how Josie will feel about us showing up."

"Then you'll just have to win her over."

"Yep." He grinned, then had a sudden recollection of their near kisses. *You can't go there, Michael. She may not even want to see you.*

He'd left Josie when she'd needed him. Had chosen his work over her. He would have a lot of apologizing to do. And, if possible, she would have a lot of forgiving to do.

He had a monumental task before him. And never before had the outcome been more important.

■ ■ ■ ■

It took Michael a month to arrange everything for their "visit" to Josie. But the wait had been worth it. He wanted to be completely relocated when he went to ask for forgiveness for leaving. He wanted her to totally trust him.

"I can't believe we never bumped into Josie the last couple of days." Lisa nearly buzzed with excitement. "I can't stand the wondering."

"No matter what happens with me, she'll be glad to see you. Remember that."

"I will."

"Hey, did you ever call Bud about getting your job back?"

"Yep. He said I could start as soon as possible. Said to show up and surprise Josie, which I want to do by myself first. I'll send a text message when we're done talking so you can surprise her, too."

"You'll be the nicest surprise she's had in a long time."

He only hoped his presence would be a nice surprise as well.

As he drove down the main drag toward the diner and passed several places that sold ice cream or funnel cakes, Michael tried to stop the memories that flashed through his mind. When he passed Dinosaur-Putt, he decided, why fight it? He replayed that miserable day of golf, which really wasn't so miserable after all. He'd almost hugged Lisa that day.

Then he passed an old-timey photo shop. That reminded him of the night he'd first realized Josie had roped him in. For the first time, he'd let himself think about having more in life.

And later when they'd laughed over dinner at Bud's? That was when he'd really dreamed of a future.

Now what did that future look like?

It depended totally on Josie.

Josie finished crushing boxes out in the back alley. She tied the bundle with a string, then hauled the umpteenth plastic trash bag into the Dumpster. Good, hard physical labor might at least help her sleep again tonight.

When she'd finished, she dusted off her hands and opened the back door into the kitchen.

And what a sight greeted her. Lisa stood with her arms in suds up to her elbows. Bud stood leaning against the sink, his ankles crossed, a crooked grin on his face.

Josie clutched her chest. *Oh, thank you,*

Lord Jesus! She's come home.

But how could that be? Had she run away again?

Lisa chattered about something. Josie couldn't hear what. Then Lisa laughed. Bud joined her, his raspy laugh sounding like a rusted door swinging open for the first time in eons.

Josie was too scared to speak. *Will she even want to see me?*

Bud spotted her and waved. "There she is. I'll let you two talk." He headed out of the kitchen, leaving a sense of dread to keep Josie company.

Lisa shook water off her hands, then grabbed a towel to dry them. Never once looking at Josie.

Josie kept her distance. "Lisa, honey, I'm so glad to see you."

Lisa turned and rushed to Josie. Tears streamed down her face. "I missed you so much."

"Oh, come here." They hugged for a minute, Josie fighting her own tears. "Can you forgive me?"

"Of course. I did that ages ago. Realized I probably would have done the same thing for a guy."

Josie gave her one last squeeze, then stepped back to take a good look. "You look great. Not a thing has changed, except you seem happier."

"I'm happier than ever."

Josie believed it. Lisa had an inner light just beaming. God had definitely been at work. *Thank you, Lord.*

"So, I take it you didn't run away again."

"No. Just visiting."

"Really?" She glanced toward the door to the diner, wondering if Mike had come. Too stubborn to ask, she said, "I hope you'll stick around until I get off work in a little while."

"I'd love to. I'll help here in the kitchen till then."

Michael walked up to the diner and stopped on the sidewalk in the dark out front. Lisa had sent him a text message a half hour ago, and he'd just gotten the nerve to climb out of his car.

The sign on the door was flipped to Closed, but the lights were still on inside, illuminating Lisa mopping the floor and Josie wiping tables, laughing at something Bud was saying as he squirted liquid across the grill.

Josie and Lisa, and even Bud. Michael's new family, God willing.

If he had never come back, he would have

left the best part of himself here in Gatlinburg. Thankfully, the Lord had brought him around.

He tested the door. It was unlocked. He opened it slowly so he wouldn't clang the leather strip of bells.

Music blared on an old radio, static and all. Bud bobbed his head in time to the beat. Lisa danced with the mop, causing his heart to swell as he noticed the same grace his sister had always had. He had another chance with this child. A chance to make the right choices this time. A chance to fulfill his sister's last request.

And Josie, his Josie . . . She carried a tray of salt and pepper shakers over to the counter and disappeared behind it.

Josie sat the tray on a shelf behind the counter. She unscrewed the tops of the salt shakers, removed them, set each one beside its shaker. All lined up just like every other day. A routine so familiar she didn't have to think at all. Which was good, since she felt more like running home and crying for a week. Lisa had come to visit. And Mike hadn't.

As she poured salt from the large container's spout to top off each one, her nose itched.

She rubbed the back of her hand over it. Then sniffed.

She could almost imagine that Mike was in the diner. His aftershave wafting in the air.

But she hadn't noticed it earlier. Not even on Lisa.

She sniffed again. Not Bud. Not her regular clientele.

Definitely Mike.

She popped up from behind the counter, upending the whole tray of open salt shakers.

He stood there smiling. "Oops. Was that my fault?"

"You don't look too repentant."

"I'm not. I'm too glad to see you."

He walked around the counter toward her. Correction — he stalked his prey.

She watched the stormy midnight-blue of his eyes the whole way. When he got within touching distance, he reached out and twirled one of her curls around his pointer finger. "I'm glad the curls are back."

"It's the humidity. There's no use fighting what's natural."

"No. No use fighting what's natural at all."

Bud turned down the radio but didn't leave the room.

"I've learned a lot over the last few weeks,"

335

Mike said. "Mainly how much I missed you."

"Yeah, well, you knew the route here." She wanted to sound tough, to put him in his place, but instead her knees felt as if they might give out. He looked so good standing there in the diner that she nearly cried.

"I did. But you see, I had a lot to accomplish before coming here. I had to get Gary promoted. To resign from some positions. And to sell my house."

She grabbed hold of the counter to steady herself. "Sell your house?"

"Yes. I couldn't keep it when Lisa and I relocated to Gatlinburg."

She looked over at Lisa. "Is he telling the truth?"

"Sure is. I'm enrolled in the school here. And we have this great house we found not too far from yours."

"You moved here, for good? Why?"

"Because you're our shoe," Lisa said, then laughed. "I'll explain later."

Mike touched her shoulder, then took her hand. "Nothing was the same without you. Our family of two was nice, but we'd be a lot happier as a family of three."

Was this really happening? Did she deserve such joy?

"I think God led us to you in the beginning," he said. "I hope you can forgive me for leaving."

The man had moved for her. Surely that proved he was sincere. *Lord, thank you.* "Yes, I forgive you. But are you sure this time?"

"Very sure."

He moved closer, hovered a breath away. She could hardly think with him like that. "What about your job?"

"It's all arranged. I'll be working from Gatlinburg."

"So this is all for real?"

He nodded. "Trust me, Josie? Me, with God's help, that is?"

She tried to remain firm when every muscle fiber had turned to spaghetti noodles. "Why should I?"

"Because I'm sorry for letting you down. And as far as is in my power, I won't ever do it again."

"And . . . ?"

"And because I miss your colorful hair."

"It's pretty bland now."

"Because I miss your curly hair."

"And . . . ?"

"And because I miss your joy in life, your bluntness, your smile. . . ."

He was practically supporting her total weight. And he couldn't get any closer without touching his lips to hers. Still, she wanted to make sure he paid his penance. "And . . . ?"

"And I may need you to hire me here if telecommuting doesn't work out."

"I could do that."

He ever so slowly leaned toward her, preparing to touch his lips to hers. "I love you, Josie. You can count on me."

"Are you ever going to kiss me, Mike?"

He seemed more than happy to oblige.

Finally, after so many moments of wanting him to kiss her, his lips touched hers. She melted into him, deepening the kiss, pouring out all the hurts she'd had while he'd been gone, all the emptiness and heartache. In its place, she let his love fill the achy, needy part inside her. She was finally home.

"What about me?" Lisa asked. "Like, where do I fit in this picture?"

He smiled in the middle of the kiss, breaking contact at the corners. "Why don't you give us a minute, here?"

She giggled. "Hey, I'm cool with that."

Bud banged on the grill with his spatula, louder than necessary. "I guess this means I don't have to kill you, Throckmorton."

"No, sir. I have honorable intentions."

"I 'spect you better tell me what they are right now, or I'll have to stop all that kissin'."

"That depends on Josie."

She grinned because she knew it was her move.

She gazed into his eyes, into his soul, to see the man she had grown to love. She knew about his strong sense of loyalty, and knew without a doubt that his loyalty, from here on out, would lie with her. And with Lisa.

Tears stung her nose. "I love him, too, Bud."

Mike's breath whooshed out. "Thank you, God."

"It's about time," Bud said. "I've had enough of her moping around here. It's hard on business."

Josie couldn't wipe the grin off her face as she and Mike stared into each other's eyes, holding hands. She couldn't imagine her life getting much better.

A soft hand closed over hers and Mike's. "So, are we going to be a real family?" Lisa looked from her to Mike, then back.

Josie thought her heart might burst to overflowing. "We already are, Lisa. We already are."

EPILOGUE

Helium-filled balloons floated around the diner. A huge Congratulations banner hung outside on the front window. Mike was so proud of Josie that he wanted to shout it out loud.

Instead, he approached her and whispered in her ear. "Miss Josie Miller, owner and proprietor." Then he kissed the new owner of Bud's Diner. "Have I told you how proud I am?"

"Yes, about a dozen times. And I still can't believe it's really happened."

"I can. You've worked hard and deserve it."

"And to think, I did it without taking a penny from you or my parents."

"Speaking of which . . ." He nodded in the direction of both sets of parents. "Should we tell them about our plans?"

"Yes, but let's tell Lisa and Bud first."

They found Lisa at the grill watching Bud

fry a hamburger. He carefully explained when to press and when to flip. Mike couldn't thank God enough for bringing all of them together. He was truly blessed.

"Hey, you two," he said. "We've got some news."

Lisa and Bud looked up from their cooking. "We already know," Lisa said. "We figured it out last night."

"Figured out what?" Josie asked.

"That you two are going to get married," she said.

Bud mashed a sizzling burger. "We're more observant than you think."

"And how did you figure this out, Mr. and Miss Smarty-pants?"

"You wouldn't get a sign made that says Josie Miller, Owner," Lisa said with a smirk on her face. "So I assumed you were waiting to get one made that says Josie Throckmorton, Owner."

"Pretty good reasoning," Mike said. "Maybe you have the mind of a banker, after all."

Lisa snorted. "No, thanks."

Bud crossed his arms. "So when's the big day?"

"What big day?" Mike's mom asked, butting into the conversation. Before they knew it, everyone had gathered around.

Mike stared into the chocolate-brown eyes of his future bride. He ran his hands through her soft hair, trying to tame the wild mess. It was hopeless. And he loved every single renegade curl.

"In exactly one hour, you're all invited to attend our wedding at the little chapel up the road."

The crowd cheered. All the noise faded into the background as he kissed the future Mrs. Josie M. Throckmorton.

"My crazy family will finally be official," Lisa said. "And it's about time."

"Yeah, Mike, it's about time." Josie laughed, all her love shining in her expression.

"Hey, I've been asking you for weeks. Don't be telling me 'about time,' you stubborn woman."

"I did say yes, didn't I?" She winked at him, then said, "Come here, Lisa." She kept one arm wrapped around his waist as she pulled Lisa into their embrace.

The three of them hugged, and Mike knew he'd never had a more perfect moment.

Dear Reader,

I love a happy ending, don't you? That's why I enjoy writing stories of love and romance. But when I threw Josie and Michael together, I couldn't imagine how the two, such complete opposites, could find happily-ever-after. No matter what the obstacles, though, in the end, love won out. When they let God lead them, they found their happy ending. And Lisa found the family and home she needed.

All of us need a place to feel secure and accepted. We all want to be loved, just as we are. Sometimes in life we don't feel we have that. But God does love us completely, just as we are. And because He first loved us, we're able to reach out and love others.

I hope you've enjoyed Josie, Michael and Lisa's story. Thank you so much for taking the time to read my debut novel. I appreciate you!

I would also love to hear from you. Please visit my Web site www.missytippens.com or e-mail me at missytippens@aol.com. Or you can write to me c/o Steeple Hill Books, 233 Broadway, Suite 1001, New York, NY 10279.

Missy Tippens

QUESTIONS FOR DISCUSSION

1. In *Her Unlikely Family* Josie is a woman who wants to be loved and accepted, faults and all. She doesn't want to be bound by the expectations of other people. Have you ever felt bound by the expectations of others — parents, spouse, friends, coworkers? If so, what did you do about it?

2. Michael makes assumptions about Josie based on her appearance. How can appearances be deceiving? Have you ever judged someone unfairly or been judged unfairly because of appearances?

3. In the beginning of the story Michael is all about business and family duty. How does that change? What do Lisa and Josie have to do with the transition? What people in your life have caused shifts in your priorities?

4. Michael, Josie and Lisa come to realize that God brought them together to form their "unlikely family." Have you ever felt

as though God brought a particular person into your life at a particular time?

5. Michael isn't sure he's capable of loving, but during the story he realizes he can love with God's help. How can we call on God to help us love more like Him? What are some practical ways we can follow Jesus' example?

6. Josie has to learn to forgive her parents and to start to heal that relationship so she can move on with her life. Have you ever had something that held you back from living your life fully? Did it require forgiving someone or asking for forgiveness? How did you make that first move?

7. We've always heard that opposites attract. Josie and Michael are definitely opposites. Do you think opposites really do attract in real life? Can a relationship like this work? What would be required to make it work?

8. Lisa needs security and a place to call home. Why do you think she finds this at Josie's house? What does Michael have to learn to help meet those needs? What can we do to help those who are looking for security and a place to belong?

9. Bud finally agrees to attend the worship service with Josie after years of refusing. What do you think leads to this? How do you share your faith with others?

10. Josie feels called to help others, like Jesus did. Do you feel God has called you in some way? How do we discern God's call? Is there something you think God has called you to, but you've been too afraid to pursue it?

ABOUT THE AUTHOR

Born and raised in Kentucky, **Missy Tippens** met her very own hero when she headed off to grad school in Atlanta, Georgia. She promptly fell in love and hasn't left Georgia since. She and her pastor husband have been married twenty-plus years now and have been blessed with three wonderful children and an assortment of pets. Nowadays, in addition to her writing, she teaches as an adjunct instructor at a local technical college.

Missy is thankful to God that she's been called to write stories of love and faith. After ten years of pursuing her dream of publishing, she sold her first full-length novel to Steeple Hill Love Inspired. She still pinches herself to see if it really happened!

Missy would love to hear from readers through her Web site, www.missytippens.com, or by e-mail: missytippens@aol.com, or you can reach her c/o Steeple Hill Books,

233 Broadway, Suite 1001, New York, NY
10279.